M000251743

THE SURVIVOR

JOHN ZODROW

Black Rose Writing | Texas

ISBN: 978-1-68433-654-8
PUBLISHED BY BLACK ROSE WRITING
www.blackrosewriting.com

Printed in the United States of America
Suggested Retail Price (SRP) $18.95

The Survivor is printed in Garamond

*As a planet-friendly publisher, Black Rose Writing does its best to eliminate unnecessary waste to reduce paper usage and energy costs, while never compromising the reading experience. As a result, the final word count vs. page count may not meet common expectations.

"This is the last text I can send. To stop them from tracking my movements, I must destroy my phone and laptop and journey in silence.

But I wanted to leave you with something my search so far has made me realize. It is that while Jesus questioned the values of society and the state, St. Paul, being a Roman, accepted the legitimacy and authority of the Roman Empire. Perhaps that is why the church over the centuries has turned a blind eye to get along with those in power. What would the world be like if Jesus had prevailed?

Hold fast. Pray for me!"

Your brother, Father Bobby

THE SURVIVOR

CHAPTER ONE

Rome, Italy

Inside the *Citta Obitorio Quattro*, Number Four of Rome's six public morgues, Burt Powell stood before the wall of stainless steel waiting for *Ispettore* Zighette to return. Beneath the smell of chloroform and antiseptic, odors familiar to him, the faint, sweet scent of death managed to tinge the air. His brother, Father Bobby, was inside one of these small square units he was facing.

Ispettore Zighette returned to the morgue, respectful, perhaps because they were colleagues, perhaps because of the horror that lay behind the closed stainless steel door. Wordless, he handed Burt a crumpled piece of what looked like flattened paper inside a clear plastic evidence baggy.

Burt stared at its message that said, "Forgive me."

"It was carved by a knife on his hand, *Tenente.*" He was using Burt's rank as a Lieutenant displayed on his badge. 'There can be no doubt of that. It is in the report I showed you."

"His hand?"

"That is his skin," Zighette lowered his eyes in shame. "His fist was clenched so it survived."

Burt had read the report written by the New Delhi policeman, P. A. Bashu. Bobby's body was found hanging beneath a bridge, badly decomposed, face, hands, arms, eaten away by rats. Perhaps, the report suggested, by crows and hawks too. There were also wild dogs or feral cats who roamed that part of the city. The report concluded that the writing discovered inside the palm of his right hand was an apology for killing himself.

"There were no fingerprints or anything else found," the Italian policeman added.

Burt said. "Let me see him."

"Are you sure, *Tenente*? Maybe you want to keep what he looked like?"

"Open it, please," Burt said.

The Italian nodded, sighed and cranked the release handle, slid the tray out and stepped back. Burt unzipped the black bag and saw a skull come into view. The animals had made close work of Bobby. His eyes were gone. Only deep, blood-stained sockets remained. Almost all the flesh had been torn from his face. As Burt stood there, looking for signs that it was his brother, he saw bits of brown hair, a few shreds of dried skin yet forming his mouth, his chipped front tooth from that time playing hockey. There was no doubt.

Bending and peering closer, Burt noticed a small round hole in Bobby's skull. "What's this?" he wondered.

The Italian leaned in and said, "Perhaps a crow pecked him. It's nothing."

"It's a bullet hole. About the size of a 9mm, I'd say."

'You cannot know that."

"Believe me, *Ispettore*, I know."

"Still the autopsy reported no trace of gunpowder, and no bullet was recovered, *Tenente.* "

"It's a gun wound," Burt said with authority. "I've seen dozens." He tenderly lifted Bobby and peered at the back of his head.

"As you can also see, *Tenente*, there is no exit wound."

"Maybe that's because Bobby does not have the back of his skull."

"Ah, yes, well, a wolf or something might have chewed it off," the Italian cop shrugged.

Fighting the desire to punch the Italian cop, Burt stepped back from his brother's exposed corpse and said, "Can I leave him here for a few days?"

"*Scuzi?*"

"I've decided not to bury my brother here in Rome. I want to take him back to Kansas with me."

"How long will you be?"

"A few days."

"*Certo.* I will do the papers myself," Zighette replied. "What will you do here?"

"Something got Bobby killed. I plan to find out what."

"I must remind you, *Tenente*, you have no authority here. You must let us handle any investigation. And now I must ask if you have brought your weapon."

"That would be illegal," Burt said. "I know the rules."

The policeman watched warily as Burt zipped the black bag shut and slid the drawer back into its refrigerated space.

"Thanks for your help," Burt said on the way out.

CHAPTER TWO

Emerging from the cold *Obitorio,* Burt stepped onto the street into the hot Roman sunlight, glad to be outside. Seeing the bullet hole had clinched for Burt what he needed to do. No matter what, he was going to bring the murderers of his brother to justice. And no Italian cop was going to stop him.

Checking his watch, Burt saw he was late for his meeting with a certain Father Martin Urrutia, a friend of Bobby's, who had left a message at the front desk of the little hotel *Angelo* where he was staying. The priest had offered information and help in any way he could on what he knew had happened to his brother.

Hurrying along *Via Ottaviano,* then onto *Via Crescenza,* he turned onto a small side street called *Maschere,* having memorized that route Father Urrutia had given him. Ahead on the corner there were a dozen white chairs and tables set out *al fresco.* He searched the area but could not locate the priest he was supposed to meet. No one was in clerical clothing. Someone tapped him from behind. Turning, Burt saw a rotund man in an expensive blue Armani suit, yellow tie, and black Gucci loafers.

"You are Burt Powell? I am Urrutia."

"Father Urrutia?" He wasn't anything like Burt had expected.

"Martin Urrutia. Yes, don't look so shocked. I stopped wearing that black stuff years ago. Very unfashionable. Sit, sit, refresh yourself." He snapped his fingers at a waiter. "Espresso is all right?"

Burt nodded—that would be fine. He didn't care what he drank or ate.

When they were seated at a small round table, Burt said, "Bobby did not commit suicide."

"No, of course not. He was murdered."

Burt's eyes widened at hearing that. "You have proof?"

Before Urrutia could answer, coffees were brought in *demi-tasse* cups, along with a plate of *biscottis*.

Urrutia replied. "You know Bobby had a lot of enemies. Even in the Vatican there are those who wished him dead."

"Why?"

"Because of what he found." Urrutia broke off as a tall nun in white robes, traditional cowl covering her face, took a seat with her back to them at the nearest table.

"Do you believe in God, Burt?" the priest asked him.

"I try."

"Even demons believe in God," the priest said as he eyed the nun.

As Burt swung toward her, she rose and quickly walked away. He thought it was an odd moment, filled somehow with a tension between enemies.

"You know her?" Burt asked the priest.

"She reminds me of *La Ombra*. a killer they call the Shadow who works for the murder for hire Fabrizio family."

"And was it her?"

Urrutia laughed. "Nothing more than my imagination. With Bobby killed, I am, how do you say, jumpy?"

A battered red Ghia swung to the curb and honked.

Urrutia said, "Ah, you better hurry, there is your ride."

"My ride?" Burt asked, confused. "To where?"

"Lola has volunteered to pick up Father Sebastiano at the train station. He arrives from Turin. You can meet him there and learn more about Bobby from him. He was in touch with him the last few days."

Burt looked at the wheezing old car hugging the curb. A dark-haired, olive-skinned young woman in denim jacket, worn jeans and short-sleeved white t-shirt that announced, "Milan Melon Festival!" swung out and yelled "You want me to get a ticket? Move it. I'm waiting."

Urrutia said in a low voice, "You can trust her. She is one of us, a friend."

CHAPTER THREE

"I am Lola Constantino," she said as Burt climbed inside. "You are Bobby's twin brother. You look just like him. Well, maybe not as handsome." She stuck out her hand. "I'm Father Bobby's friend. Or was."

"Burt Powell." He shook her slender hand which was surprisingly dry and cool and noticed she chewed her fingernails. Even though she wore too much make-up, especially heavy around the eyes, she was very pretty. Burt wondered just what relationship Bobby had had with this lovely thing.

As if reading his mind, Lola said, "Father Bobby was my *professore*. I wasn't screwing him."

"I never said that."

"No, but you thought it."

By his embarrassed expression, it was obvious he had.

In her rattling and battered 1973 Ghia, red paint peeling, left fender crumpled, front bumper missing, Lola swung violently out into traffic and cursed a smoke-belching truck as he narrowly missed her, honking loudly. "Hey, b*astardo. Testa di merda.*" she swerved in front of a taxi.

Burt hanging on, said, "I got B*astardo. Testa di merda?*"

'Shit head." She snorted contemptuously. But he saw her eyes nervously sweep the rear view mirror. Her expression reminded him of the long look that Father Urrutia had thrown the nun.

"I learned to curse on the streets of Napoli," Lola said. "A shit hole of a town, corrupted by mafioso, ruined by your United States Navy. Father Bobby arranged a scholarship to the university. I owe him a lot. He got me out of there."

"*Mannaggia. Vacagare.*" Lola flipped off two Vespa riders who cut in front of her. One kicked her front fender as he passed.

"*Mannaggia?*" Burt waited for the translation.

"Damn."

"And the other?"

"What did I say? I can't remember."

"*Vacagare?*"

"Piss off."

"Quite a vocabulary."

"Maybe I'll teach you." Lola grinned. "You look like you need to express yourself more. It, how do you say, comes with the territory for me. In Napoli, you learn to take care of yourself. No one in Italy loves that city. I hate it too. Every street owned by a different Don making shopkeepers and ordinary people pay his monthly *pizzo* for protection so they won't get their shops and homes burned down. It is a city of garbage piled on the streets, noise and despair. Drugs sold in *piazzas,* ancient fountains empty of water, littered instead with syringes. And all the time, old killer *Vesuvio* ready to blow again and burn them all. "

She never stopped talking, diving through tiny holes in traffic that only a cat could squeeze through. "So what are you doing here?"

"I want to prove Bobby was murdered."

"And then?"

"And then get the ones who did it."

Lola, impressed, nodded. "Okay, then look, you need to know a few things. Father Bobby found an ancient document in the Vatican archives. He said that it was extremely important to keep it safe."

"Safe?"

"You repeat yourself like some idiot? Yes, safe from the Hand of Christ, a bunch of radical right wingers. Bobby thought they would do anything to get it back, even kill him."

Burt studied the young woman. So close to Bobby, she clearly was someone he needed to get to know better. Someone who knew things. "Did he tell you what the document was about?"

"It was part of what we had been researching." She pulled out her iphone and tossed it into his lap. "Press S," she said.

He did and a photo of a semi-naked, bearded, long-haired man, hands modestly crossed on his abdomen popped up. He peered at the photo. The long sheet of cloth showed both the front and back of him.

"You're looking at the Shroud of Turin. Tell me. With your cop's eyes, what do you see?"

He ignored the insult. "Looks like a dead man."

"Really? See if you are smart enough to see what your brother did."

Burt grunted at the challenge. "All right. I'm looking at feet, hands, chest, all showing what looks like holes."

"Those are wounds. You see blood stains too?"

"I don't know. Something is coming out of his wounds."

"That's blood. Can a corpse bleed? Any pathologist will tell you you need a live heart to pump blood. Once death ensues, circulation ceases. "

"Alright, so what?"

"So that is what your brother was investigating when he found the ancient document in the Vatican archives called the *Yuz Asaf.*"

"The what?"

"Are you deaf? The *Yuz Asaf,* it's Arabic!"

"Okay, what does the *Yuz* whatever mean?"

"It revealed that Jesus never died on the cross. That backed up Bobby's conclusion on the Shroud."

"And this is what you think got him killed? I mean, c'mon!"

"C'mon, yourself. Father Bobby was terrified because he knew if this was true, then the Church was a fraud and the world's history and future would be changed forever. There would be no Resurrection, no Redemption of man's sins, no immortality of the soul. And Christians everywhere would suffer a devastating blow to their faith and belief."

Realizing, Burt let that sink in. "And so Bobby set out to find the truth."

"Or, as he hoped, to disprove it ever happened."

Burt said, "Either way, the Hand of Christ could not gamble on what he found."

"*Certo*! Even for a cop you are very slow."

"I admit it doesn't quite fit the real world I'm used to living in."

Slamming on the brakes so hard it nearly sent Burt through the windshield and made him clutch the iphone, Lola double parked in front of the *Intermezzo* train station. Snatching back her cell, she rolled out, leaving the Carmen Ghia blocking part of the street.

"They'll give you a ticket!"

"I hope they tow it!" she shouted over her shoulder.

They went up a flight of stairs and emerged into the *Porta Stazione Nuova di Roma* The train station was filled with passengers arriving and departing, porters carrying luggage, and trundling heavy carts filled with shipped cargo. Long lines of rail cars stood behind locomotives. Lola quickly checked the big board and said, "We're late. Father Sebastiano has arrived on Track 19. Hurry."

Trotting quickly down the platform, Lola spotted a white-haired priest, in a black suit. After greeting him and kissing Lola on both cheeks, the priest turned to Burt, "*Tenente* Burt Powell? I am *Padre* Sebastiano. You may call me Aloysius." They shook hands.

The priest picked up his single black bag. But Lola grabbed it from him.

"I can carry it, Lola."

"I will carry that, Father."

As they walked, Padre Sebastiano said to Burt, "This is a sad time, is it not? I have prayed unceasingly for Father Bobby's soul."

"Just what was your relationship with my brother?" Burt asked.

"I was his superior at the Collegium di Santa Maria which is part of the Inter University Center for Comparative Analysis of Institutions, Economics and Law. We perform all manner of investigations. Nothing is off limits. As you say, anything goes."

A locomotive's shrill whistle blew as it chugged past them, pulling cars from the station.

"Father Sebastiano," Burt asked, "do you know where Bobby was going?"

"I do not know his final destination," Father Sebastiano shook his head. "Only that the last place he spoke to me from was Tarsus. Tarsus, Turkey."

The nun in white whom Burt had seen at the *ristorante,* now strode toward them. Withdrawing a 9 mm Glock, she shot Father Sebastiano. A little girl nearby, witnessing Sebastiano's head disappear in an explosion of bone and gore, screamed in horror.

Lola dropped the suitcase and grabbed Burt's hand, jerking him away. The nun fired again at Burt hitting him in the skull. He stumbled and fell.

People all around on the platform panicked and began to run. Coolly, *La Ombra* pushed forward, determined to make sure of her kill. But passengers blocked her path. To make matters worse, two *carabinieri,* alerted by the commotion and screams, spilled out of a blue and white police station.

Lola shielded Burt, screaming at *La Ombra, "Sei una puttana inutile!"*

The nun hearing the insult, glared at the young woman, but was forced to retreat. She leaped down off the train's platform onto the tracks below. The *carabinieri* fired at her, but she boarded a nearby passenger car that was waiting to depart.

Inside, *La Ombra* located a restroom, entered and locked the door. She tugged off the nun's white habit, revealing beneath a priestly black suit and roman collar. Glancing in the mirror, Delicata Fabrizio, which was her real name, smiled and thought she made a handsome man.

Outside the bathroom, one of the *carabinieri* ordered the other to go forward and search the car. He tried to open the bathroom door, and found it locked.

"Open up!" he commanded.

The door burst open and a blond, crew-cut priest in a clerical black suit looked out. The young priest looked genuinely startled at the gun in the cop's hand.

"*Scuzi, Padre.*" The officer apologetically lowered his weapon, then raced past the priest through the car filled with passengers nervously waiting to depart.

Clutched in her hand, hidden behind the bathroom door, *La Ombra,* held the 9mm Glock in case she had been forced to kill the cop.

Now she stepped back inside the bathroom, unscrewed the silencer from the Glock and shoved the gun inside the holster beneath her arm. Re-emerging, she glided casually down the train car's steps onto the platform, looking like she did not have a worry in the world. In the milling crowd, she began searching for what she always called her pigeons. Even in the chaos of people fleeing and screaming, there was plenty of time to finish the assignment given her by The Hand of Christ. Known in the trade as the very best at what they did, Fabrizios did not give up easily.

CHAPTER FOUR

Burt and Lola stumbled through the panicked throngs into a side exit of the train station. Burt staggering, bleeding profusely down the front of his face, caused people to stare. To hide him, Lola took off her blue jacket and draped it over his head. Police with sirens blaring were arriving from all directions. Out in the parking lot, she pulled Burt down behind an old Mercedes just as several policemen ran past. Yanking out her cell phone, she screamed something unintelligible in Italian, then disconnected.

"How bad is it?" she asked, looking at him.

"I'm alive," Burt mumbled, obviously dizzy and in pain.

Lola lifted her coat and checked. "She missed. Well, sort of."

He tentatively felt the gash with a finger. "It's not deep. "

She looked again. "Do you part your hair on the left?"

"The right."

"It will be on the left now."

In the distance came the whelp-whelp cries of even more approaching sirens.

"*Porca miseria.* They're going to close off the station. We have to hurry." Lola pulled him from behind the Mercedes, then down steps, toward a busy street below.

"Lola." Burt yelled as they fled. "We should talk to these guys. They're cops."

"Do you want to die? That nun will kill you."

Two blue uniformed, white-belted Italian police spotted them. *"Alto!"* one ordered.

Lola ignored the command and yanked Burt into an underground pedestrian tunnel that ran beneath the street. They were just steps ahead of the *carabinieri*. In the darkened subterranean tunnel, Burt saw that the overhead lights had been smashed out by vandals. Lola grabbed hold of his collar and swung him into a small alcove. Red, white and yellow wires dangled from the wall.

"A phone booth." She explained." Like most in Rome, wrecked. Not needed with everybody having cell phones."

They were pressed tightly together in the narrow space. Her face inches from his, breath soft on his lips. Even wounded, he felt the warmth of her breasts and stomach against him.

"I don't have one," he said.

"One what?"

"Cell phone. I did but when the battery went dead I forgot to charge it."

She hesitated, then relaxed into him. "How long ago was that?"

"Two, three years."

"You are, how do you say *primitivo*?"

"Primitive, yeah, I guess. I like the old fashioned way in most things."

The moment broke as the cops raced by, not seeing them in the darkened alcove. Their footsteps receded.

"Nice move hiding us here," he whispered.

"I grew up on the street, remember?" She gazed up at him. "The bleeding has almost stopped."

He leaned out, bracing himself against the cement ceiling. "I think they've gone."

Turning, he saw tears in her eyes. She swiped at them with her wrist. "I just thought of him. Father Aloysius was a good man."

"I'm sorry I didn't get to know him." Burt said, then added, "That nun was pretty good."

"*La Ombra.* Definitely not Mother Teresa."

"Sent by your friendly Hand of Christ. But I keep wondering why this hired killer was after me in the first place?"

"Maybe because you are a cop and Bobby's brother? Maybe you told somebody you were here to find out who killed him?"

"I did mention that to a fellow officer. But he seemed like an okay guy."

"They all appear okay guys. You should be more careful."

Burt said, "Again, what if I wasn't the intended target. Maybe she was after you and just missed."

"Me? Why?"

"Well, she shot Father Aloysius because he knew things about my brother."

Lola snorted. "I was only Father Bobby's assistant. He wouldn't even tell me where he hid the *Yuz Asaf*. Said if I knew it would put me in danger."

"Maybe the Arabic document was a phony, you know, just made up. Something concocted by Islam or somebody."

"The Muslim religion began in 610 AD. The *Yuz Asaf* was written by historians over 500 years before, in 33 AD."

Burt thought a moment. "Okay, but what if this killer somehow thought you had that document? That would make sense to kill you."

"Well like I said, I don't have it. And I don't know any more about it. Now shut up about the *Yuz Asaf.*"

Burt startled at her overreaction. But the sound of a blaring car horn made Lola turn away and peer out into the tunnel. "About time," she said.

A silver Rolls Royce slammed up next to them. The driver's window whirred down and Father Urrutia peered out.

"It took you long enough," Lola scolded him.

"I had to circle the train station."

"When I called, I told you we would be in the tunnel."

"I know, I know. But those *polizia* were suspicious. Where is Father Sebastiano?" He appeared alarmed.

"The nun murdered him."

"*Ah, dio mio, santa maria de atoche.*" Urrutia crossed himself in dismay.

Lola jumped down from the phone alcove into the tight space of tunnel and car and managed to ease open the back door.

"Father Aloysius dead." Urrutia shook his head. "And look at you, Burt. You, you've been hurt too. Are you alright?"

Two pistol shots echoed behind them from the mouth of the tunnel shattering the back window of the Rolls. Turning, they saw a priest fire again.

"Who is that?" Burt dove into the back seat, pulling Lola with him.

"*La Ombra!*" Urrutia blasted the Rolls forward, crunching a fender. More slugs smacked the vehicle's trunk as they roared out of the tunnel.

He drove fast and in a few minutes, they arrived on the outskirts of Rome, zipping through neighborhoods of apartments with clothes drying on lines, passing open weed-filled fields. Turning onto a one lane service road, he stopped. From the back seat, Lola and Burt saw a sign announcing *Ostia Nova Aero Puerto.* Urrutia lowered the driver's window, and reached out to run a plastic card through a reader. A gate arm raised up in front of the car and the priest floored it toward a sleek private jet, parked at the edge of a runway.

Arriving at the jet, Urrutia got out and scanned the area, his expression grim. "We have to be alert," he said. "These nut cases are dangerous."

"What are we doing here?" Burt wondered.

"You know, it occurred to me that Father Aloysius saying Bobby was at Tarsus makes perfect sense."

Burt said, "It is the last place we know Bobby was at."

"But he died in India," Lola protested.

"Yes," Urrutia said, "but to understand why he went to India, we must find out what he was after in Tarsus. And believe me, when it comes to beginnings, everything about the church started in Tarsus."

He pulled out his cell and typed in a number. The plane's door opened and boarding steps unfolded.

"Who's flying this thing?" Lola started to enter.

"Why, me, dear girl." Urrutia's cell beeped. "And now our flight plan has been filed."

Jauntily, the fat priest bounded up the stairs after Lola and Burt, then retracting them, he latched the door.

"Best buckle in," he said.

They each took one of the four leather swivel chairs in the spacious cabin as Father Urrutia flung himself into the pilot's seat and started the engines.

Expertly swinging the jet's nose around, he began taxiing toward the runway, all the while revving the twin engines. He radioed the tower, received permission for take-off, then pulled the levers back. The jet lurched forward pinning them in their seats with its huge thrust.

Once in the air at cruising speed, Lola asked Urrutia if there was a medical kit aboard.

"Rear head!" he shouted.

She told Burt to follow her. In the rear restroom, she located the Medical Emergency kit. Opening it, she used ear swabs and hydrogen peroxide to clean out the half-inch long gouge in his scalp.

"A little lower," Lola observed, "and you wouldn't be here."

"She might have finished me off except you made her mad. What did you scream at her?"

"Oh, that? *Sei una puttana inutile?*" she shrugged noncommittally. "It means she's basically a fucking whore who can't shoot straight. You want a bandage on that?"

Burt grinned and shook his head. "No, but I will take some penicillin if there's any."

Searching the kit, Lola found a bottle of tablets.

After Burt finished swallowing three of them, he picked up Lola's jacket which was caked with his dried blood. "I'll buy you a new one."

She threw it in a trash can. "It was an old thing. Don't worry about it."

Burt washed his face, neck, then took off his stained shirt and bare-chested, scrubbed away more of his blood.

For a moment, Lola's eyes dropped to his stomach which was flat and hard. Then she caught herself. "You need a new shirt. I'll see if Urrutia has something."

She went up to the cockpit and in a moment returned with several.

"What size are they?" Burt was wiping his face.

"Not extra, extra large, if that's what you're worried about."

"Then they're not Urrutia's," he smiled, choosing a teal-colored t-shirt with a small insignia of *Monaco* embroidered over the pocket.

"Fashionable," she approved as he slipped it carefully over his head.

Returning to the cabin, they now found Father Urrutia behind a small bar, making drinks.

"Ah, you look most dashing," Urrutia admired his shirt.

"I'll have it cleaned and returned."

"Forget it. My friend lost a fortune wearing that last time in Monaco. He doesn't need to be reminded. His name is Borg Anslander, my tournament bridge partner. This is his plane. Martini?"

"I'll pass," Burt said.

"Make me two," Lola smiled. "Your friend must be doing well."

"Borg makes ball bearings. Lots of little stainless steel balls. His company's motto is 'We Make the World Go Round.' A generous man. Loans me his plane. Taught me how to fly too."

"Uh, speaking of which, who's flying it now?" Lola looked alarmed.

"Oh, that would be my assistant, Otto."

"Who?" Burt looked around for someone he had perhaps missed.

"Don't worry," Urrutia laughed. "Otto, as in autopilot."

CHAPTER FIVE

One Month Earlier
New Delhi, India

Emerging from the air-conditioned Indira Gandhi International airport, Father Bobby Powell, in full priestly black suit and white collar, stepped uneasily outside onto the sidewalk into what felt like a wall of hot water and prayed what he was about to do would not cost him his immortal soul.

Despite the sweltering heat and humidity of summer in India, he had dressed purposely this way so the man he was going to meet would recognize him. After checking around to see if he'd been followed, he went to the taxi line and picked out a three-wheel auto rickshaw. Alighting into its small rear cab, he then told the driver he needed to go into the old part of town. The *tuk-tuk* operator quoted him a price, then darted the flimsy contraption out into the tangle of traffic, dodging honking trucks and buses, whipping past shouting street hawkers selling flip-flops, workers eating bowls of cooked rice and fish with bare hands, slowing for wandering sacred cows, the streets full of businessmen in suits, pretty women in *saris* hurrying among high rises and always the squatting poor outside their makeshift tents huddled on sordid, stained sidewalks.

The air was so polluted with vehicle exhaust that Bobby had a hard time breathing. He was flung from side to side as they madly drove through crammed intersections, past white-gloved traffic police, mocking Mercedes limos filled with plump rich behind air conditioned, tinted windows.

After a few miles, the driver thankfully slowed somewhat and swung off the main boulevard. Now, the *auto wallah* guided his *tuk-tuk* into a tighter, quieter, older section of the city, filled with little winding lanes and alleys. Blowing his horn to alert pedestrians, he snaked the little green cab past sour-smelling booths selling everything from eggplant pickles to perfume.

Sweating profusely, Father Powell prayed to God to forgive him for what he was about to do. For the umpteenth time, he questioned his motives in seeking the truth about the *Yuz Asaf* document he had discovered. If he found that it was true that Jesus did indeed survive the cross, how many believers would abandon their faith? Perhaps millions.

And yet, and yet, he always returned to the same conclusion. Let the truth out. Open the windows as Pope John XXIII had said. Let the facts speak for themselves. It was time for the church to quit living a lie. The world was owed the truth, not a fabrication. Still, in his heart of hearts, Bobby secretly prayed that at the end of his quest, he could disprove the document and show that it was false.

A gargantuan white marble temple loomed up ahead. Its facade and walls were adorned with thousands of carved gods and bare-breasted goddesses. He recognized it from photos. The ancient *Nili Chhatri* temple. This was the place. Father Bobby asked the taxi driver to stop here and wait for him.

Climbing up the worn, stone steps, he entered the vaulted Hindu temple dedicated to Lord Shiva, welcoming its cool interior. Above he saw soaring walls covered with Hindu goddesses, writhing in dance, coupling with well-endowed male gods. On the floor, sitting along the walls beneath the carvings were the real, flesh and blood mortals, diseased and crippled, their hands out, begging. He handed out the last of the rupees he had exchanged. Children, playing with a soccer ball, ran merrily past as he seated himself on a bench next to an open arch, from which he could view the square below. This was the scheduled meeting place.

In a few moments, an Indian in a white *halaba* appeared. Obviously nervous, he spotted Bobby and furtively made eye contact with him. Then, cautiously, the Indian came up into the temple.

When he was close, he whispered. "I am Kali. Kali Mohi, the janitor."

Bobby smiled at that. That was the key word they had agreed on. In Latin, "janitor" meant the "keeper of the key." Exactly what the Indian's duty represented.

Kali pulled a white envelope from his tunic.

"What's this?" Bobby wondered.

"The proof. Of all that the *Yuz Asaf* revealed."

Bobby refused to take the envelope. "No, Kali. Our deal was I could go with you and see the proof with my own eyes."

"It is too dangerous now." The Indian warily checked over his shoulder.

"But I've come all this way, Kali. We agreed you would take me there."

"You don't understand. I'm being followed." the Indian whispered, his voice shaky. "Take this. Run away. Now." He put the envelope into Bobby's hand. "Please. You..." the Indian tried to speak but instead his eyes opened wide. He uttered a small cry of surprise then fell to the temple's stone floor.

Father Bobby bent to him. Kali's blood was spreading on the cobblestones, pooling beneath his head. Mystified, he turned him over. There was a gaping hole in the back of his skull. The beggars and children who had seen Kali fall, hurried away.

A shadow covered the priest.

Looking up, Father Bobby saw a beautiful Japanese girl with enormous dark eyes, breasts pushed up brazenly over her blouse top, her long, slender legs, exposed beneath a very short school uniform skirt. She held a pistol with a silencer in her hand.

The girl cooed sweetly, "My name is Iva, the sad *anime* girl of God."

Bobby was so astonished at seeing this odd vision, that it took him a moment to realize she wore the plastic mask of a smiling animated waif. The *anime* girl pointed to the envelope the Indian had given him.

"Please hand that to me, father?" She raised the pistol.

Bobby leaped to his feet and fled from the temple.

Turning into a narrow cobbled lane, he spotted a battered red Royal India mailbox, hanging lopsidedly on a wall. It gave him a desperate idea. Stepping inside a nearby stall filled with bags of curry, he withdrew a pen from inside his clerical jacket. As the proprietor of the booth watched silently, he scribbled a name and address on the envelope.

Ducking down as the smiling girl passed by the booth, he murmured a prayer to God that someone would pay the postage, and raced back to the mail box to slip the envelope inside.

Darting into another narrow alley, he turned checking but did not see her pursuing him. With a feeling of relief that he had escaped, Bobby suddenly realized that this street was a dead end. To his dismay, he stood facing a closed, wooden door. He lunged forward and tried the handle. It was locked.

Quickly he turned to retrace his steps, but the sexy young girl appeared, blocking his way.

He hammered on the door, calling for anyone inside to help him. "Open the door." he cried. "Please. Help me!"

Someone inside shouted, asking what he wanted.

"Prepare to stand before Almighty God," the cartoon-looking girl said.

Turning, Father Bobby saw rather than heard her fire the silenced weapon.

CHAPTER SIX

Malta

Island of Gozo

Beneath the San Paolo cathedral, in its darkened basement, Cardinal Giuseppe Montalvo sat waiting impatiently with Monsignor Anselmo Tuppo. A month ago, the Monsignor, Master of Vatican Archives, had requested an immediate solution to an urgent and sensitive issue. An ancient and important document had been stolen from the Vatican Archives. The thief was known, a certain researcher named Father Robert Powell, specializing in Pre-Christianity studies, that dark period between the time Jesus died and the first writings explaining he was Christ the savior were produced by St. Paul.

Above the two clerics, a Mass was being celebrated and they could hear the sanctuary bells ring and the choir sing the "*Sanctus, Sanctus, Sanctus*" in the old, outlawed Latin still performed on Sundays in this ultra-conservative parish in Malta.

"Anselmo," the Cardinal said. "I want to warn you."

The Monsignor leaned his ear close from where he stood behind the seated prelate.

"Do not react to what you will see. Do not say anything when she arrives, understand?"

"What will I see?" the Monsignor asked uncertainly.

"She wishes to startle, to be outrageous with her appearances," Montalvo said vaguely. "It is best to say nothing."

As if by magic, at that exact holy moment of consecration, of turning bread and wine into the Body of Christ above, the door silently swung open and a woman in a tight red dress, model tall, in very high stiletto heels, with long legs exposed, entered. Her hair was a flaming red. In the light of the single naked bulb hanging from the basement's ceiling, she moved like a cat, slipping into the chair before the Cardinal's desk, keeping her face, modestly bowed.

Cardinal Montalvo congratulated her, "Another clever disguise, Delicata Fabrizio."

"That is what my family is known for, Eminence." Raising her face, she smiled. A lovely Rita Hayworth. But the smoldering glare in the huge eyes of Angelina Jolie. It made Monsignor Tuppo involuntarily take a step back.

He knew that for over two hundred years the Fabrizio family, ostensibly owning groves of olive trees high in the hills above Palermo, had carried out contract assassinations. A long line of Fabrizios had been engaged by politicians, men of commerce, wealthy individuals and the Church itself to annihilate their enemies. And during all that time, not one Fabrizio had failed an assignment. In addition, none had been arrested, much less tried. The reputation of the Fabrizio family was impeccable. If, Monsignor Tuppo thought, you considered a pack of sociopathic, psychotic killers as approaching any kind of perfection.

Behind him, the Cardinal heard Monsignor Tuppo clear his throat nervously. "And just who are you today? A movie star, I take it?" he asked with a smile.

"A movie star with something special added, Eminence. You see, in New Delhi, I was an innocent *anime* girl, fresh from the *manga* comics. Today I am a shemale, complete with a long, fat correct cock between my legs. Would you like to see?" Delicata opened and closed her legs in anticipation.

"How impure, how wicked," Monsignor Tuppo muttered under his breath.

The Cardinal sighed, then smiled back at Delicata. "Will you perhaps take some *grappa,* daughter?" He reached and un-capped a wine decanter.

"No, *Grazie, Eminencia,*" Delicata shook her head. "I do not drink."

"Tell me then, Delicata, how is your brother, Massimo?" the Cardinal, making small talk, inquired politely. He knew that this woman was steeped in sin. Despite being a hired assassin, Delicata had for years slept with her brother and was deeply in love with him. And he wished to put her off balance and not allow her savage nature to rule this meeting.

Delicata's eyes narrowed but her voice fell flat as she said in a monotone, "Massimo is in North Sudan, working for the Chinese. There is a problem with their oil refinery there. It seems they have no oil to process. The South is not delivering it. It is being worked out."

"Ah, yes" the Cardinal said, understanding that Massimo was there to kill the opposition, "And I pray that soon Sudan has the oil to trade for weapons from China. It is an evil thing, but better than dying."

Delicata shrugged dismissively. "At this moment, they have a choice. But not for long."

Cardinal Montalvo continued his apparently courteous inquiries, establishing his authority. "It has been many years since I worked with your father. I trust Umberto is well."

"He suffers from Alzheimer's. At times, he does not recognize even me, *Eminencia*."

"A shame," Montalvo teased out the string. "And yet, perhaps it is a form of God's mercy."

"How is that?" Her voice was deep for a woman but now she sounded a bit off balance.

"So he will not remember his many victims and therefore his numerous sins?"

She sat up, her back straight, raised her face into the harsh bulb light and behind the long lashes, Montalvo saw that her eyes had softened. She whispered, "Every night I am home, my father asks me to read aloud each name of those he conquered. He listens and is very proud of his victories, *Eminencia*."

The Cardinal nodded and heard Tuppo shuffle impatiently behind him. Satisfied at her response, Montalvo now turned to him. "Monsignor, shall we now proceed back to our little problem?"

At that cue, Monsignor Tuppo stepped a little forward into the single bulb's light, deliberately averting his eyes from Delicata's long, crossed legs and said, "Please report. Have you recovered the dangerous document that was stolen from the highly confidential *Riserva* section of the Vatican Archives?"

Delicata, instead of looking at Tuppo, continued instead to stare at Cardinal Montalvo. "The *Yuz Asaf*, was not on the priest in New Delhi. I searched him thoroughly."

"What happened to it then? Did he hide it somewhere before coming to New Delhi?"

"I do not know. I know only that he received an envelope from the Indian man he met in the bazaar. And when I searched the priest later, even that was not on his person."

"Is it possible that the envelope he received from the Indian contained the *Asaf?*" Tuppo asked.

Montalvo frowned, deep in thought. "Yes, he might have sent it to him."

Delicata recrossed her long legs. "I believe it was something else in the envelope."

"But what?"

"I do not know. And besides that is not my job to know such things."

"Perhaps Father Powell left it with someone, a shop keeper, in the bazaar?"

"I offered them rupees. The shop keepers are dishonest. They would have produced information for money."

"At any rate, the fact remains that you failed," Tuppo announced harshly to her. "The *Yuz Asaf* document taken from our Vatican library is still missing."

"Now, now, *Monsignore,*" the Cardinal smiled. "I am sure there can still be success. The Fabrizios are not known for failure."

"We have no time to waste!" Tuppo shouted. "God only knows at this very moment who has this heresy in their grasp. If our enemies get hold of it and it emerges say on the Internet, or God forbid, is published in a book, a magazine, the Church stands to be ruined. We are wasting time, Eminence. Does this woman not realize that if this conspiracy succeeds, the very credibility of Holy Mother Church is at stake?"

"Monsignor Tuppo," the Cardinal said to Delicata, "though he is agitated, does not exaggerate. The revelation of this invidious document would send shock waves throughout Christendom. Think clearly, Delicata," the Cardinal urged her. "Recall everything you saw. Perhaps there is a clue."

"I remember when the priest ran, he carried the envelope the Indian handed him. And..." she stopped and frowned.

"Yes?" the Cardinal urged.

"I passed a mail box. It was hanging crooked on the wall."

"Perhaps then he put the envelope in the mail?"

"But he had no postage." Delicata said.

The Cardinal thought a moment, then turned to Tuppo. "Find out the policy of the Indian postal service for unstamped mail. Use that marvelous little cell phone of yours to find the answer, Anselmo."

Tuppo went on Google and typed in the question.

"I understand it is your plan to kill Father Aloysius and the woman Lola at the Rome train station," Montalvo said to Delicata. "Is that a good place to do it?"

"I like crowds," she said. "Easier to escape."

"But easier also to kill bystanders."

"Collateral damage sometimes happens," she shrugged. "Don't worry. I know the Hand of Christ's orders. Their entire nest will be wiped out."

Monsignor Tuppo closed his cell phone. "India follows the same postal rule for unstamped mail as does Great Britain."

"No surprise there," Montalvo said. "Colonial rule."

"They deliver the letter it is addressed to and collect the postage due."

"Then the letter was sent, regardless of postage. But who did the heretic priest mail it to? And what was in it?" Cardinal Montalvo stood and held out his ruby ring which Delicata kissed. "Use all your wiles to find this *Yuz Asaf* and rid us of these betrayers of Holy Mother Church."

She rose and left. When she had gone from the cellar, the Monsignor shuddered distastefully, "*Che feminina!*"

"To protect Holy Mother Church, we use who we must," the Cardinal replied. "As for Delicata, may God have mercy on all who face her!"

***

Ebbetsburg, Kansas

The tornado had come up from Wichita and in the darkened morning hours miraculously leaped and bounced willy nilly over the small town of Ebbetsburg, leaving some buildings, randomly destroying others, finally squashing Mrs. Callahan's big red barn. The barn had, for several centuries, been the most notable thing about Ebbetsburg, famous only for its wheat fields and sheep farms.Burt Powell eased his cruiser off the highway and followed the path the twister had left, always amazed at how it rolled up barbed wire fences and gathered them into giant barbed-wire balls. Ahead, on what they called a hill in Kansas, he could see the remains of what was once the barn he had known since he had been a boy. Played in it many times as he grew up. He and brother Bobby shooting each other with rubber bands, taking turns dying realistically as they had seen in films. "Was that realistic?" each would ask as chests were clutched, mouths open in anguish, feet flopping on some Texas town's dusty main street where the latest rubber band showdown had been imagined as they tumbled down into piles of hay. Prizes were awarded for the most realistic dying in the form of penny candies—equally shared regardless of winner.

Angie Happens walked toward him as he pulled up carefully, trying not to put a tire on a nail, or sharp edged board torn from the barn's foundation, now strewn about in scattered wreckage. He always thought Happens was a silly name, something made up. But Angie was no mirage. The tautness of her officer's shirt across her well-tuned chest made her very, very real.

He rolled his window down, "Angie."

"A mess, huh?"

"Well, not as bad I hear as up in Wichita. Mary?"

"Oh, she's alright," Angie adjusted her utility belt and hitched her .45 up higher on her slender hips. "Said she was in the shower when she heard the thing coming. Thought she was a goner. But you know Mary. Said, what the heck I came in naked, might as well go out that way too."

Burt nodded. "Tough lady."

"Settled these parts, with her husband, John."

"Jacob."

"What?" she leaned closer to the window to hear in the wind.

"Mary's husband was Jacob."

"Oh, yeah. I get them mixed up sometimes. John's her boy."

"He been notified?"

"On his way from Denver as we speak." Angie swung back to the sight of the ruined barn or what was left of it. The Ebbetsburg fire department, in the form of two volunteer sixty-something fire fighters, their secondhand fire wagon parked nearby, was checking for cans of gas, other combustibles.

"Well," Burt said, "I guess I'm going back into the office. Seems you got things under control here."

"Sure, thing," Angie said. "Hey." She smiled and leaned farther into his window. "We going bowling tonight?"

He looked up at Officer Angie Happens and saw despite her physique that she constantly worked at with exercise, she was aging. Lines cut ovals on both sides of her mouth. Frown lines too. Deep ones. But there were still laugh crinkles at the corners of her eyes. And when she smiled now, still sunshine.

"Right as rain."

"A few beers. Coupla laughs. All the while I kick your skinny cop's ass."

"You wish. I'm feeling frisky. Got my new ball yesterday, arrived from Amazon."

She leaned closer and he could feel her warm breath on his face as she said, "Frisky, huh? Well, save that for afterward."

"Can't stay the night," he said. "You know tomorrow is Francie's anniversary."

"Gotta take her flowers," she said sourly.

"White roses. She always loved white roses." He stopped and said, "You know, I miss her."

Elmer Neal pulled up beside them in his patrol car, the third and total number of cruisers owned by the Ebbetsburg Police Department. In the back seat, there was a young girl, maybe twelve years old.

"Dilly Masterson?" Burt saw her look at him.

"Ran away again," Angie nodded.

A Ford 150 pickup swung in behind Elmer's cruiser and a short, bearded man with stubby fingers rushed and tried to jack open the back cruiser door. But it was locked.

"I warned Stabler not to come around her," Burt said angrily as he swung out of his squad car.

Angie warned him. "Stay out of it. It's a Children's Service matter."

"Service. That's an odd way to describe that institution." He strode over to Stabler who was beating on the back window of Elmer's cruiser, shouting, "You get in the truck with me, right now!"

"You're not my father!" Dilly screamed at him through the closed window. "I don't have to do what you tell me to."

Burt arrived and said, "Step away from the car, Mr. Stabler. I am ordering you to step clear, sir!"

"She is my lawful ward and I am taking her back," Stabler swung at Burt who ducked and threw a straight arm punch into his nose. Rudolph Stabler fell backwards onto the ground.

"You, you, you broke my goddam nose!"

"I'll do more than that if you get up, or assault a police officer again," Burt said. Then turning to Elmer, said, "Unlock the door, Officer."

Elmer released the lock.

Burt opened Dilly's door and said softly to her, "Honey, I thought we fixed it so you wouldn't have to run away again."

Dilly, staring hatefully at Stabler who lay on the ground, clutching his face, said. "He came back."

"He was bothering you again?"

Dilly nodded, looking ashamed.

"What about your mother, Irma?" Angie interjected, having walked to the cruiser. "What's her part in all this?" She already knew the answer to that, but wanted to make Dilly say it out loud in front of Stabler.

"She pretends it don't happen, ma'am. She don't see a thing."

"That's a goddam lie," Stabler muttered without conviction. "Nothing's happening."

Burt crouched down and faced Dilly where she yet sat on the back seat. "I can put Stabler away if you press charges against him."

Dilly bit her lip, thinking. "If I do that, my mom won't have enough to rent the trailer. She told me that. What she gets with food stamps and welfare ain't enough."

"It's the only way out," Angie told her. "Sometimes you just have to stand up for yourself and change course."

"I can't do that. I can't do that against my mom."

Burt said, "Elmer, you go on and take Dilly home."

"You sure about that, Lieutenant?"

"Right as rain, I'm sure." He said to Dilly, "Sweetie, you can go on home now. There's not going to be any more of this with Stabler."

"How can you say that?" Dilly eyed him doubtfully.

"I promise, you, I promise you that. Things are changing now. It's all going to be different. Do you trust me?"

She hesitated, then looking mystified, nodded her head. "Alright, if you promise."

"That's a good girl," Burt said. "You are a good soul. You didn't do anything wrong here, Dilly. You are a wonderful person with a bright future. You are a beautiful, fantastic girl and you will grow into a good woman as well. You believe that?"

For the first time, she smiled.

Smiling back, Burt closed the door. Elmer got into the driver's seat and started up the cruiser.

Stabler jumping to his feet shouted, "You'll get what's coming to you when I get home! You'll see, you little bitch! Causing all this commotion. Got my damn nose broke!"

When the cruiser with Dilly in the back drove away, Burt said, "Stabler, walk with me."

"I ain't going nowhere with you." He started back to his pickup.

Burt grabbed Stabler by the scruff of his shirt collar and yanked him toward the barn wreckage. Angie lit a cigarette.

Stabler screamed at Angie, "You gonna let him do this? I'll lawyer up on you!"

When they had come behind scattered pieces of roof tin and torn beams, Burt said to Stabler, "Now don't say a thing. Just listen. I know you. I knew your worthless, no-good daddy. I know your whole thieving, lying family. So pay attention to what I'm going to tell you. "

"You can't talk to me like this. I got rights. You're a law officer. You can't do this!" Stabler screamed at Angie who still had her back to him. "You gotta treat me right. I got my rights! I'll sue your department for treating me like this."

Burt got close to Stabler's ear. "Rudolph, I'm not talking to you as Officer Burt Powell. I am speaking to you from the part of me I keep hidden. It's a character flaw I developed during the two wars I fought in Iraq. You see, my job was to go out at night and wreak havoc, make the enemy shit their pants. I'd creep up into camps of sleeping *mujahadeen* and slit their throats. Cut their heads off. Just like they were doing. But I always left one barely alive to spread the word I was there and would return. And here's my promise to you, Mr. Stabler. If you so much as go near Dilly or her mother Irma, if you so much as drive by the front of their house, I will kill you. That's not a threat, Mr. Stabler. It's my war oath."

"You can't..." Stabler looked scared.

"Shhh," Burt said. "Now here's the rest of the deal, Rudolph. Man to man. I want you gone. I never want to see you around these parts here ever again. Tell you what, I think you ought to head to someplace nice, like Canada."

"Canada?"

"Don't even need a visa to go there. You're American. They like Americans up there. Well, sorta. Maybe some place like Calgary. Yeah, I gotta friend up there, an ex-cop, he'll keep an eye on you. Don't try to run from him. He'll find you. He's gotta a bad rep for a short fuse, wears big cowboy boots he uses for stomping. He's mean, Rudolph. Meaner than you. Probably why the New Orleans police department forced him out. Now, don't even bother to go back to the Masterson trailer to pack your things. Just leave right now with the clothes on your back. Call me from the Wichita airport after you've bought your ticket and again when you get into Calgary. You can call collect from Calgary and I'll accept the charges. I want you to call me every day for the next month so I know you're still up there. Oh, and leave that pick-up of yours in the long term lot. I'll send somebody to get it. Irma will like the use of that. And that way, Dilly won't have to take the bus to school anymore."

"I ain't giving you my truck," Stabler whined.

Burt slapped his face hard. "You're not listening. If I ever hear you left Canada, or God forbid show up anywhere around Irma and Dilly Masterson's trailer, I will do you on sight. That's a solemn oath. Is all that crystal clear, Mr. Stabler?"

"You..." he stammered through split lips, "what about Irma? She needs my disability I get." He tried to grin, showing he had the advantage. "How about that, big shot? You mess with me, you gonna take away their livelihood."

"I already thought about that," Burt said. "Not to worry. I will personally take care of them. Dilly and Irma don't concern you anymore. Now, climb in your pickup and drive away. Because after today, if I lay eyes on you, I will fulfill my oath."

Stabler stared at him, his eyes hardened into tiny points of hatred.

"You know," Burt said, "I just realized something. Since you are a child molester, I won't kill you right away. I'll put you in a dark hole somewhere, keep you alive for a long time. Cut off your balls, your fingers, your toes, bleed you upside down like hanging a hog for slaughter."

Stabler started to protest. Instead, he lurched toward his Ford 150, started it, and with the tires flinging mud, swung around and headed down the road. As he passed, Burt stared at him. Stabler looked away.

Angie walked to Burt and said, "You didn't do something I don't want to hear about, did you?"

"It was all very amicable. Mr. Stabler has offered to move away."

"Where'd you send this one?"

"Calgary."

"Calgary. Whatever made you think of that?"

"I got creative."

"You know he won't go there. None of them listen. First, he'll run just like all the other criminals you sent away. Stabler's got cousins down in the Ozarks. Probably head there."

"Point is, he won't come back here for a while."

"And when he does?"

The car phone in the cruiser beeped. Burt opened the door and heard Wally Topper, the dispatcher in their Ebbetsburg office, say, "Burt? You got a call come in for you here."

He reached in for the mike. "Some kinda emergency?"

"Well, I don't rightly know. But it's long distance, from somewhere called Tureen, or something like that. Says it important."

"Patch it through." There was a moment of static, then what sounded like clicking sounds and a man with a foreign accent said, "I am trying to reach Lieutenant Burt Powell."

"This is Burt Powell. Who is this?"

"You are military, Lieutenant?"

"I'm a police officer, sir. What's your business?"

"I am Father Aloysius Sebastiano, superior at *Torino* University."

"Torino? University?" Burt couldn't focus.

"As you say, Turin. It is in Italy. This is about Father Bobby. *Signore, prego?* Perhaps it is better I tell you this when you are ready."

"Ready for what?"

"It is bad news, very bad. Perhaps I should write you. Perhaps it was a mistake to call like this. But Father Bobby gave your number to call in case something happened. You are his brother, no?"

"We're twins. What did you say your name was?"

"I am Father Sebastiano. Father Bobby's superior here at the University."

"Why are you calling like this, Father? Did something happen to Bobby?"

"Something more than terrible, Burt, may I call you Burt?"

"What is it, Father.?"

"You are *Catholico*, Catholic, Burt?"

"I'm not anything. Maybe I guess, born Protestant. Bobby converted."

"I only ask because of the importance of what I must tell you."

"Is Bobby hurt? Is that what you are telling me, Father Sebastiano?"

"More terrible than that, Burt. Father Bobby is dead."

The mike sagged below Burt's mouth and rested on his thigh. Angie reached in and squeezed his arm. "Oh, Burt," she said. "I'm so sorry."

He did not move for a bit, then forced himself to recover and said to Father Sebastiano, "I just talked to him last month."

"They found his body. He was hanging from a bridge in New Delhi."

"Where? In India?"

"That is correct."

"On a bridge? In plain sight? Bobby hung there? What was he doing in India?"

"I was told the bridge is in a part of that city where there are garbage filled streets, hovels, many poor. Bodies in the street and all around are common. The police do not patrol there. A charity picks them up once a month. That is how they discovered Father Bobby."

Burt swallowed and said, "Why did you ask me if I was Catholic?"

"Because of how your brother died, Burt. I was afraid to tell you, but I was more afraid if you are Catholic."

"And why is that, Father? What could make it more terrible?" He made himself concentrate on the jumbled pile of useless, shredded barn wood, torn apart like a human muscle, tendons striated and exposed.

"Father Bobby committed suicide. And for a Catholic, that is a grave sin. I was only trying to prepare you for that additional shock. Normally today, most of the times, the church allows one who takes his own life to be buried in holy ground anyway for reasons of not being in his or right mind. But there are three reasons when one cannot. If you are a notorious apostate, a schismatic, broken away from the church, or a heretic who holds doctrines contrary to the church, you are banned from a holy burial. In Father Bobby's case, a local bishop who is a member of a very conservative faction in the church, has forbidden him to receive the rewards of a faithful priest. He has concluded he was a heretic, and a manifest sinner to whom a church funeral cannot be granted without causing public scandal to the faithful. I don't agree with him, but I am powerless to change his decision."

Burt took a long moment, then turned away from the devastation of what was once a barn he loved and played in as a boy. "Where is Bobby now?" he asked. "Where's his body?"

"It is being brought to Rome."

"I don't understand," Burt said. "I don't understand any of this. But I will tell you one thing that I am absolute certain about, Father."

"Yes?"

"My brother, Father Robert Mark Francis Powell, did not take his own life."

***

With his flight out in the morning to Rome, Burt stayed in the area around the Ebbetsburg Estates trailer park that evening and hid in the recesses and shadows of several big oaks. To his disappointment, about ten that night, Rudolph Stabler drove his Ford pickup in front of the Masterson's trailer and slammed on the brakes. Looking drunk, he angrily kicked the door open and stomped inside, shouting at the top of his lungs that he was back and what did the two of them think of that? There were the sounds of things thrown and curses screamed. Then the front door was thrown open and Dilly ran out, pursued by Stabler.

Quietly, Burt circled back and flanked them, a move he had performed a thousand times before, coming in directly behind Stabler. Snaking his arm out, he caught Stabler around the throat and with one hard deft motion pulled him behind a massive oak trunk. Dilly, sensing her pursuer was no longer behind her, slowed. She watched in the moonlight as Burt muzzled Stabler with one hand over his mouth as he struggled uselessly in the policeman's arms. With the other he cinched off the blood flow to his brain, quickly sending Stabler into unconsciousness.

Dilly darted back to the trailer where her mother was calling from beneath the porch light. In a moment, the single door slammed and a dead bolt latch was fastened, securing it.

***

In the morning, as Burt left his house with his single piece of carry-on luggage and hurried to his Jeep, Angie was waiting.

"Your truck's muddy."

"Been down by the river."

"Cemetery and Francie's the other direction."

"Just tying up some loose ends."

"Don't worry. I'll watch the house for you." She decided not to pursue the conversation.

"Thanks," he hugged her. She kissed him on the mouth. A movement that made him startle from the grim thoughts he yet entertained. He forced himself to smile briefly for her and started to say, 'Don't worry. Just going down to the corner store to get some chewing gum.' But he stopped himself. It was what he had always told Francie when he was called up to report to Iraq. His hero the astronaut John Glenn had said to his wife that same thing whenever he had to leave for a flight into space. And she would reply, "Don't be long."

Instead, Burt waved and drove away.

CHAPTER SEVEN

Present Time

The Small Airport Ostia Nova Aero Puerto

Outside Rome

Following the Rolls Royce in a taxi, *La Ombra* arrived at the small airport Ostia Nova and watched the cop, girl and priest board the private jet then take off. It did not matter. She would catch up with them. Calling a traffic controller who was a member of The Hand of Christ, she requested the recently filed flight information on the Gulfstream jet and was told its destination was Tarsus, Turkey. Purchasing a commercial flight ticket on her cell phone, *La Ombra* ordered the taxi to continue onto Fiumicino airport.

Once there, she boarded the plane that would take her to Incirlik, very near Tarsus. In an hour, landing at the NATO airbase, she emerged from the flight, still dressed as a priest, and headed past hundreds of arriving NATO and American soldiers, most heading to or on leave from, nearby Iraq.

Several said, *"Padre"* or "Hi, Father." as she passed them.

Ignoring the rental car agencies because it would leave a trail, she surveyed the crowded airport. Turks in 10th Air Wing uniforms. American Air Force with their 39th Air Base Wing insignias. She didn't want a struggle with these young bucks so she patiently waited for an older soldier to pass by. An American Major with his silver leafs, in a blue Air Force dress uniform trundled out the door. Overweight, balding, his hands thin. A bureaucrat. Even the halting way he moved told her he was a desk jockey. An older animal in the herd and the most vulnerable.

La Ombra trailed the Major out to the parking lot.

From a short distance, she watched him find his car, a green Toyota. As he opened the trunk lid to stow his luggage, she came up behind him and asked, "Can you give me a ride, Major? I'm afraid I don't have enough money in our church budget to rent a car."

The officer smiled, seeing the priest. "Where'd you come in from, Father?"

"Roma. San Ignacio. I have come to give a retreat."

"Well, Rome, huh? Where you heading to?"

"San Angelo parish. In Adana."

"I can take you as far as the base, guess you can catch another ride from there, if that's alright."

"I'm not picky."

"You have any luggage?" the American asked.

"It was lost by the airlines."

"That's a shame. Hopefully they'll find it."

"God willing."

The Major stuck his hand out. "Major Danby."

"Father Fabrizio," *La Ombra* shook his hand. "Are you Catholic?"

"Used to be. Sometimes I think maybe I should get back to it."

"You should," *La Ombra* agreed, climbing into the passenger's seat.

They drove out onto the main highway.

The Major said, "I just got in from Baghdad, heading home tomorrow, back to my wife and our kids and grandkids. Been here flying in cargo and personnel for over two years. I can tell you, Padre, I am one anxious Texan, ready for stateside."

The priest listened politely and after about several miles traveling down the highway, said to the Major, "I'm sorry, but I have a problem."

The Major looked over solicitously.

"I should have used the bathroom."

"You gotta go, you gotta go." Danby said.

"You can pull off anywhere here," the priest said. "It won't take but a minute."

The Major spotted a little side road and swung his Toyota Camry off the four-lane highway. Pulling behind some trees, he stopped.

"There," he said, "this oughta afford you some privacy, padre."

But the priest did not move.

The Major frowned, not understanding. "Padre? You goin' or what?"

The priest said, "Do you remember your Act of Contrition?"

"Beg pardon?" the Major looked confused.

"You should say it now."

"I… c'mon, Padre, what's going on?"

"I can help you if you don't remember it. It begins, 'O my God, I am heartily sorry for having offended Thee...'"

"Look," the Major interrupted. "I don't know what you're doin' but this ain't regular."

The priest withdrew a 9 mm Glock and pointed it at the Major.

"What the Sam Hill?" The officer recoiled in surprise.

"I like you, Major. I'm giving you a chance to tell God you are sorry for your sins."

The Major said, "Why don't you go fuck yourself."

La Ombra shot him in his right nipple.

He grunted as if hit by a baseball bat. Then managed with surprise on his face, "None of this makes any sense..."

"I tried to help you," *La Ombra* told him. "But you refused God's grace."

"You're a weirdo," the Major gasped. "That's what you are." He made a sudden lunge for the gun. But *La Ombra* fired another slug into his chest.

The Major recoiled and stared in shock.

"Normally, I would shoot you in the head or heart. But I want your lungs to fill with blood and not stain the driver's seat. I have to sit there."

The Major's dimming eyes said he thought she was mad.

"Oh," *La Ombra* cooed softly, "a little blood will seep out. But it won't be splattered all over. Easier to clean that way."

Gore bubbled up and frothed over Danby's lips, then flowed out his nose onto his tie and white shirt front.

She waited patiently as life left the Major and when he slumped against the side of the car, quickly got out, crossed behind the Toyota, jacked open the driver's door, and let him fall onto the ground. Checking the highway, she quickly dragged the American into a thicket of trees.

Climbing back inside, *La Ombra* started the Toyota Camry, turned it around and drove back to the highway.

CHAPTER EIGHT

Mersin, Turkey

Before landing at the small Mersin airport, Urrutia had arranged for a liveried chauffeur to pick them up.

"Nice ride," Burt said, seeing the waiting Bentley as they de-boarded from the jet.

The driver politely introduced himself. "I am Wezo," he said in broken English. "Please enjoy the bar's refreshments."

Urrutia told the driver to take them to Mithra's temple in nearby Tarsus.

"Yes," Wezo said, "It is only fourteen kilometers away. We will be there shortly."

The Bentley floated like a boat on its soft springs out of the airfield, then entered the D020, the main four-lane highway that ran clear across Turkey. Urrutia pulled out the sliding lid on the rosewood bar and spotted the silver shaker already prepared at his orders with condensation dripping off its side.

"The martinis," Wezo smiled. "I made them myself. Very dry just like you requested, Father."

"Thank you, Wezo. Ah, yes, proof there is a beneficent God." After Lola and Burt demurred, he poured his first martini into a tall frosted glass.

"So why did Bobby come here to Tarsus?" Burt asked.

"Because of St. Paul. He's the focal point of what your brother was working on. You see, the saint was born here in Tarsus, a Roman citizen."

"So why Paul?" Burt wondered.

"Less than twenty years after Jesus was on the cross, he was being forgotten," Lola said. "His apostles were arguing with each other over what Jesus's message was. Nobody could agree on it. And to make matters more complicated, Peter was trying to keep Jesus for Jews only, while Paul wanted to take him out into the gentile world. It was a mess."

Rolling over the ancient Roman-built Justinian bridge, they crossed the swift flowing Berdan River, Wezo pointed out dozens of Turkish wooden sailboats called *gulets*, unchanged for thousands of years, laden with cargo which was lashed on their decks, bound for other ports.

"So," Urrutia continued, "Paul, who knew about the pagan god Mithra and his church, began to write his Epistles, using a theology that resembled Mithra's "savior theology, but making Jesus savior to the world."

"What about the gospels?" Burt wondered. "Didn't they explain who the real Jesus was?"

"Don't forget they came much later after Paul's epistles. Mark's was the first," Lola said, "then Luke, followed by Matthew. All those three gospels came twenty to thirty years after Paul's Epistles. And Mark and Luke were Paul's disciples. Both of them, like Paul, never met Jesus. Matthew was the only gospel writer at that time who knew Jesus and he worked with St. Peter. His gospel was probably more truthful, but many scholars believe Matthew's gospel ending was added later to include the Resurrection.

"Only St. John's gospel was left to really explain what happened to Jesus the man. And his wasn't written until 80 and 120 years later. It again reflected Paul's interpretation of Jesus as the savior of mankind."

"So John got it right?" Burt put it together.

"Scholars believe John is not the sole author of that gospel. And that early church fathers inserted that Jesus was the Christ, the savior of mankind who died for our sins."

"So Paul won," Burt said.

"Big time," Urrutia agreed. "Later, even more so when Constantine made Christianity the official religion of the Roman world and even made Jesus Christ into Mithra the warrior, depicted in armor, holding a sword."

The car traveled past women in black *burkas,* the ankle length modest dress for Muslims. Ahead of them, men in long white *dishdashas,* strode separately while their donkeys carried baskets filled with corn, tomatoes, avocados, apricots, oranges.

Leaving town, they entered the countryside, passing neatly tended farms with fields of abundant green crops of maze, corn, alfalfa and cotton, all being harvested by tractors made by John Deere and Caterpillar. In another mile, Wezo swung off the highway onto a small dirt road. Up ahead, two Doric Roman columns rose high above a stone temple, built into the side of the hill.

"Ah," the driver said, "The temple of Mithra." They climbed out of the car and stood around what appeared to be a charred fire pit.

"This could be where Bobby made camp. Look, a tent was set up over there." Urrutia pointed to half a dozen stake holes in the ground.

As they started up toward the mouth of the cave. Burt asked, "I still don't get the connection. Why did Bobby need to come here to Mithra's temple?"

Urrutia chuckled. "See if you can guess who I am describing. Born of a virgin on December 25. Three Magi following a star brought him gifts. He was called the "good shepherd," "the way, the truth and the light," "redeemer," "savior", "Messiah" "son of God." He was human, yet divine. Had twelve disciples and performed miracles. He was identified with both the lion and the lamb. He was crucified and died to atone for the sins of mankind. Buried in a tomb, he rose from the dead on the third day. And returned to heaven. His religion was organized into a church with a developed hierarchy. With a Pope who wore a sacred miter on his head. His principal festival was Easter, celebrating the time of his Resurrection. Anything sound familiar?"

Burt said, "The answer's obvious."

Lola said, "Wait, you should hear more. His church had seven sacraments, including the "Eucharist", a sacred meal of bread, water and consecrated wine. He said, 'He who will not eat of my body, nor drink of my blood so that he may become one with me and I with him, shall not be saved.' His religion had a Baptism to wash away sins. Sunday, "the Lord's day" was sacred. His religion taught there was an afterlife, consisting of heaven and that you must be virtuous to be admitted with the other beatified there. That there was a hell peopled by demons, situated in the bowels of the earth. That the soul is immortal. That at the end of time, there would be a resurrection of the dead and in a last judgment, after a conflagration of the universe, he would reward and punish every soul."

"What's the big deal?" Burt shrugged. "That's Jesus Christ and his Church."

"Is it?" Urrutia smiled. "You see, we were describing the pagan religion of Mithra."

As Burt frowned in confusion, the trio stepped from sunshine into the gloom of the temple. Pausing to let their eyes adjust, Urrutia snapped on a flashlight he had brought.

"That's better," he said as they pushed deeper into the darkness.

"After Christianity became the official State religion of the Roman Empire," Lola continued, her voice echoing, "Mithra's temples all over the world were systematically desecrated and destroyed. The largest Mithraic temple in the world was located on Vatican hill. It was ransacked and burned down by rampaging Christians who murdered Mithra's followers. St. Peter's basilica is built on top of it."

Urrutia pulled out a long-nosed .45 revolver.

"Don't worry." he said. "I always carry Junior." "There could be wild animals or even criminals living here. If this temple is like many of the others, there should be an altar deep inside, with corridors that offshoot down to seven different levels. The deepest were reserved for the most highly initiated. But we won't go down there. With its many tunnels, we might get lost."

After a few feet, a stench of rotting garbage assaulted them.

"Whew." Lola said. "Somebody's been dumping in here."

"Maybe even bodies," Urrutia grimly joked.

They picked their way inside, venturing deeper into the three-thousand-year old, stone cavern, the light from the sun eclipsing totally behind them, leaving only the dim beam of Urrutia's flashlight. Passing more piles of refuse, red-eyed rats scurried away in its beam.

"It's freezing in here." Lola shivered. She could see their breaths steaming. Burt jumped as hundreds of shiny black beetles scuttled up a stone wall.

Everyone's shoes were squishing on the mud floor. After a few minutes, Urrutia swung the beam to one side and illuminated what appeared to be a side cave.

"Here." He strode into it and Burt and Lola followed. After about a football field's length, his light found what looked like a shattered altar. As they drew closer, a faded fresco depicting a young man holding a knife, wearing a Phyrigian cap, like the French had worn in their Revolution appeared above it. The man was slicing a black bull's throat.

"Who's that?" Burt asked.

"The god, Mithra." Lola announced.

"Yes," Urrutia added, "In this depiction, you see, Mithra is the sun, overcoming the bull, which is darkness."

Moving the beam higher, Urrutia shone his flashlight on a crumbling stone cross. "They even used the cross as their symbol. It was the sign of Mithra. His followers actually carved a permanent cross on their foreheads."

Next, Urrutia lowered the beam to reveal footprints in the mud. "I wonder if these could be Bobby's?"

They tracked the steps further until they emerged in a higher ceilinged cavern. There above a larger and more intact altar, was a water damaged, ancient mosaic of a smiling, radiant-looking young man holding a staff with a halo around his head.

"If I am right," Urrutia said, "here is what Bobby came to verify."

"He looks like Christ," Lola said.

"Precisely," Urrutia agreed. "Or maybe Christ looks like him, huh? Even St. Augustine admitted that Mithra and Christ were the same. Paul erased Jesus by overlaying Mithra on him. Your own Thomas Jefferson called St. Paul the 'destroyer of Jesus.' And among many scholars weighing in on the subject of St. Paul and Mithra are Friedrich Nietzsche, Sigmund Freud, Carl Jung, Soren Kierkegaard, Rev. Charles Biggs, Franz Cumont, Martin Luther, Thomas Jefferson, Martin Luther King, Christian Father Manes, Thomas Paine, to name just a few. All have come to the same conclusion that St. Paul invented Christianity. St. Paul made Jesus disappear forever, even taking Mithra's church with all its infrastructure, and making it into an instant version of hierarchical and theological Catholicism."

"In addition," Lola explained, "the early Church destroyed fifty-six gospels that didn't fit Paul's narrative. Only the canonically approved gospels of Mark, Matthew, Luke and John were allowed to remain in existence. Still, monks disobeyed the church and hid some of the gospels, including that of St. Thomas and Mary Magdalen which have survived today."

"By the way," Urrutia chuckled, "the Latin saying attributed to Jesus, "*Ego sum via, veritas et vita*" meaning: "I am the way, the truth and the life," ironically first came from Mithra.

Gazing at the ancient mosaic of Mithra, Lola asked, "This dates from what time?"

"At least six hundred B.C. Possibly earlier." Urrutia told her. "The halo verifies that Mithra was holy and that he was called 'Truth and the Light,' 'Redeemer,' 'Savior,' 'Messiah,' 'Son of God,' the 'Lion and the Lamb,' and 'Risen From The Dead.' It is bizarre that in transforming Jesus into the Christ, Paul even used Mithra's attributes word for word, rebranding a humble Jesus into Savior and Redeemer of all mankind. Got to give Paul credit. He was one hell of a marketing genius."

"Father," Burt asked. "A personal question. If you believe all this is what happened, how do you handle it?"

"Me?" Urrutia smiled. "The original Jesus is who I believe in. He's enough for me."

Something large snuffled behind them along the cave wall.

"What was that?" Lola turned.

Urrutia swung the light but they stared uncertainly into the blackness, seeing nothing.

"We should leave," Burt suggested.

"Good idea," Lola started out.

Urrutia panned the flashlight back toward the entrance but the beam browned and sputtered. "I should have checked the batteries. Perhaps we should move fast before we lose the light entirely?"

As they walked, the only sounds were the sucking noises their shoes made slogging through the slime on the ground.

Burt said, "Alright, if I'm following everything you both said, it doesn't matter if Jesus lived or died. Either way, Paul transformed him into this guy Mithra. So why did Bobby come here? I mean, what did Mithra's cave tell him?"

"Theologically, I think Bobby wanted to know if Jesus *had* to die for the sins of mankind," Urrutia said. "Of course, he didn't if St. Paul just made the whole thing up."

"So," Burt thought it through, "if it wasn't *necessary* for Jesus to die and save mankind, then he could live."

"Brilliant theorem," Urrutia exclaimed. "And the proof of that conclusion is that Father Bobby did not return home and give up the search. What he found here made him continue on."

"But where did he go next?" Lola asked. "Direct to India from here?"

"I think there is more he was after," Urrutia said. "More that he needed to know."

A loud growl behind them interrupted more conversation. Urrutia swung the flickering, yellow light around to reveal a dozen filthy, muddy dogs. Hearing a dog howl in pain, they saw in Urrutia's meager light, that the biggest cur was biting the others.

"What's he doing?" Lola looked alarmed.

"Trying to egg them on to attack," Burt said.

The flashlight died and they were thrust into total darkness. Urrutia swung and fired the gun blindly at the wild dogs.

A ragged beast lunged and grabbed Lola's pant leg. She screamed and Urrutia fired again, the blast echoing deafeningly in the cave. This time the slug found flesh and a dog howled in pain.

"Hold hands and run." Burt said.

They reached out and found one another.

"Don't let go."

"Nobody fall."

***

Outside Mithra's temple, Wezo, the limo driver, grew bored and turned on the car radio. The station was playing some modern Turkish music from the distant capitol in Istanbul. Very chic and loud. The words were racy too. Those Muslims in the north were not close adherents to the faith, but rather Secular, loose in observing the laws of the Koran. He listened as the woman sang promiscuously about taking a man's face and placing it between her breasts.

Wezo felt his member stiffen. Catching himself, he sat up straighter and checked around, making sure his clients were not approaching to see him in this state. When someone tapped on his window, he jumped. It was a woman, wearing a modest tan-colored Muslim *burqa*, her face hidden behind mesh.

Turning down the radio, Wezo zipped down the window. "What do you want?"

The woman did not reply. Instead, she opened the mesh veil. The woman's eyes were strange. They looked right through him. Like he wasn't even here.

The woman raised a pistol and shot Wezo.

La Ombra pulled him out. She had arrived in the Major's Toyota about a half hour ago, ahead of her schedule. When at last the chauffeur had driven out of the little airport at Mersin, she identified her particular targets in the back seat of the Bentley and had followed. Trailing them to Mithra's temple, she saw them enter but decided she would not yet go into the darkened cave. It was better to wait here, outside, in the light for them to return, then take them there. Parking the Toyota in a grove of olive trees just above the cave's entrance, *La Ombra* settled in to wait for her pigeons to return.

Her cell phone buzzed. Annoyed, she wondered who would be calling her now. Then she saw on the caller ID it was her brother Massimo. But it was not his voice. The reception was tinny. A man with an Indian accent, echoing over loudspeakers. "Last month, India's parliament was asked to invest $750 million with China and Malaysia in this proposed Sudan oil pipeline. It is blood money, used by the Islamic National Front to buy more arms and kill its people."

"Can you hear him?" Massimo asked.

"Who is he?"

"A South Sudan big-wig. His speech is being carried live on a BBC broadcast. I'm about a mile away but I have him in my sights."

"Tell me more." That feeling of adrenaline and sexual excitement she loved was growing in her belly.

"I am using a .50 caliber Barrett M82A1."

"Is it good?"

"The latest and best. I will let you shoot one when I return."

"Will your pigeon hear it?"

From the time they were children, they had played this game. With their mother dying during Delicata's birth, brother and sister had formed a special bond. Both knew what the Fabrizio family, their father and uncles, did for a living. And so, even as children, it was natural that they practiced their trade in small ways. Massimo would strangle a sparrow, a mouse and watch Delicata's eyes, seeing how she reacted, enjoying it. Pigeons were always their favorites to catch and kill, and after they took up their professions as adults, the name stuck.

"No, he'll be gone before the sound gets to him."

La Ombra shivered with pleasure.

"It is so powerful it doesn't matter where the bullet hits." Massimo's voice was lower now, almost a whisper. "It literally tears an arm or leg completely off. A head will explode like a melon."

"Say when," Massimo told her. "You are pulling the trigger."

Delicata Fabrizio closed her eyes, picturing the Indian Parliamentarian, crooked her finger and pulled. "Now," she whispered.

A shocking blast exploded from her cell phone sending an electric wave shock from clitoris to breasts.

La Ombra opened her eyes. "Where did you take him?"

"In the chest. He blew apart in a dozen pieces. People are running in panic everywhere. Soldiers around the stage area are uselessly firing their Kalashnikovs at nothing."

"You promise you will show me how to use such a gun."

"When I return. I will give you more than my gun."

Her cell phone disconnected.

CHAPTER NINE

To their relief, a dim, ghostly luminance reflected ahead on the black, wet, rock walls.

"The entrance." Burt shouted. They rushed forward, the sunlight growing brighter.

"We're there." Lola cried. "We made it."

At the entrance, they spun to see the dogs were gone. Breathlessly, they fled out the temple's mouth, until they were standing between the two marble Roman columns, in glorious, warm sunshine.

"I never want to go back in there." Lola could not stop shaking. "What a horrible place." She stared at her mud-caked shoes and jeans. "Just look at me."

"Wait." Urrutia said, staring down at the Bentley, "Something's wrong."

Burt and Lola looked down at the limousine. Behind the steering wheel of the governor's limo, sat a Muslim woman in a *burqa*.

"Where's Wezo?" Urrutia asked.

"Stay here," Burt told Lola. He and Father Urrutia hurried down to the car. The veiled woman in the driver's seat did not move. As they drew closer, Burt and Urrutia could not see her face through the mesh.

"Get out." Urrutia jacked open the door. "Whoever you are." The woman did not react. He reached inside and pulled down the cloth from her face, then reacted in horror as the chauffeur's lifeless body tumbled out and fell on the dirt.

From behind him, a voice said, "Normally, I would offer the chance to repent. But with you, I don't believe it would do any good."

Urrutia spun to see a tall, close-cropped blond wearing Wezo's chauffeur livery. "Who are you?"

In a blur, the assassin fired expertly into Urrutia's mouth. The shocked Basque, revolver only half-raised, dropped to his knees.

She swung next to shoot Burt, but he was already rolling on the ground. As *La Ombra* popped off two rounds, he leaped up and kept zig-zagging back up to the mouth of the temple where Lola yet stood, frozen.

The assassin started up the hill toward them.

Burt grabbed Lola's arm, pulling toward the cave.

She resisted. "Oh, no, I'm not going back in that place."

"We have to."

"I can't. The dogs, the dogs will tear us apart."

"It's our only chance."

The assassin fired at them, the smooth marble stone above their heads fragmenting.

Lola reluctantly allowed herself to be pulled back into the wretched cave.

Running, Burt said, "What did Urrutia say about the levels in here?"

"That...the corridors led to seven different...no." Lola realized what he was suggesting. In growing terror, her stomach turned over. "Stop! I'm not going further!" And she pulled away from him.

Stopping, Burt said, "Down. That's where we're going. Down." He yanked her forward. "We'll go all the way to the bottom if we have to."

"Are you nuts?"

A bullet whistled over their heads.

"*Puta! Bocchinara!*" Lola screamed at the killer.

They both ran as the sunlight completely vanished behind them, the cave once again totally dark. They could her the killer's shoes crunching behind them, closing in.

"Look," Lola said, "she has Urrutia's flashlight."

In the blackness, they saw the light briefly shine then die. The killer shook it repeatedly, then cursing, threw the flashlight down.

"Surprise!" Lola shouted. "The batteries are dead, you stupid *fica*."

La Ombra fired in their direction.

Burt pulled her forward and yelled, "Now we have her."

"Have her? She's got a gun. Burt, I can't. I can't do this."

"You didn't act like this before when we were in here."

She gasped, keeping up. "Because, alright, because, I'm claustrophobic. I'm terrified of tight places. I can't stand to even be inside a closet. I held it together before. But I can't now." She squeezed his hand in desperation. "Burt, my legs, I can barely run. Maybe, maybe we can hide and she'll just pass us by. I mean she can't see either, right? I really can't do this." Her voice was choked with emotion.

Gun fire spewed from the barrel of the assassin's gun. A bullet whistled over their heads.

"*Porca miseria,*" Lola hissed.

"What's that one mean?"

"Bloody hell."

"A little mild for the situation!"

"*Caccati in mano e prenditi a schiaffi!*"

In answer, three slugs whined into the rocks above them.

"Wow. What did you say?"

"I told her to shit on her hands and rub it on her face."

"Nice. Feel better?"

"No. Yes. A little."

Burt had one hand out in front, feeling along the wall.

"What are you doing?"

"It was somewhere along here. I've been counting our steps like I did before when we came in here."

"You were counting? And?"

"At my 184th step, I felt a breeze, a draft."

"You were counting." It wasn't a question.

"Trained to do that. So I could find my way back behind enemy lines at night."

"Back to where?"

"My base. Now, hold onto my shoulders so we don't get separated. I'm going to use both hands to feel the wall."

Taking the lead, Burt moved in the dark, feeling his way, inching along. Lola, hands on his shoulders, followed.

"I almost forgot. Where are the dogs?" she had the terrible thought.

"Gone, I hope."

"You're just saying that to make me feel better. Right?"

"Right."

"Tell me they're never coming back."

"Okay, they are never coming back."

"Maybe they ate each other," she whispered hopefully, taking blind steps behind him. "Maybe they're sleeping. Worn out. Maybe..." Each step she took, she expected the dogs to attack.

They shuffled along in the dark for another fifty feet or so, then another bullet ricocheted off the wall and whined away.

"She's closer." Lola ducked down as she walked.

From behind them an unexpected light appeared. Both swung to see the killer, not a hundred feet behind them, lift a lit cigarette lighter into the air. Its flame illuminated her as she squinted forward.

"She's got a light." Lola said.

"I just thought of something. What about your iphone?"

"*Broccola, cazzara, allocca.* I am so stupid." Lola fumbled in her jeans and pulled out her cell. Opening the lid, she turned it on and in its dim blue light, smiled at Burt.

"I don't know why I didn't think of it."

"You were a little stressed." In the phone's glow, he said "We're at step 187. It should be here."

Lola swung around. "The dogs! Listen! They're close! I can hear them breathing."

"Wait I can feel air. This way!"

Peering hard in the dim light from the iphone, Burt could just make out a passage with a flight of stone steps descending far below out of sight.

"Get inside." Burt commanded.

Lola peered down the darkened stairs. "No way.

Dogs or no dogs, I'm not going down there."

"We won't have to if you take your jeans off."

"What?" she looked confused.

He was already undoing his own belt, removing his trousers. "It's our only chance."

Still not understanding, she unbuttoned her Levis and hopped out of them.

"Get over on the other side of the doorway."

In the meager light, she watched him tie their pants legs together, then lay the trousers just below the first step so they were out of sight.

Holding onto one end, he handed Lola the other and took a position opposite her. There was just enough room against the walls for them to stand hidden.

"When I say 'pull', yank as hard as you can."

They waited as the killer approached, her lighter growing brighter.

La Ombra stopped. She could hear them whispering. She fired the Glock in that direction. But she did not hear a cry of pain. She raised the lighter she had found in the chauffeur's pocket. Its dim orange flame bent. From her left, a draft of air. Was it coming from a tunnel? Raising the cigarette lighter high, she saw that there was indeed an entrance. A doorway. Where did it lead? She advanced cautiously, holding the quivering flame in front of her, gun pointed, ready for anything. This could be a trap, she told herself. The pigeons could be waiting. Hesitating, *La Ombra* heard a low growl rattle the rock walls behind her.

Swinging the lighter around, she saw in its glow a dozen, mud-caked mongrels, yellow fangs bared, mouths dripping saliva.

La Ombra shot the lead dog. The rest of the pack sprang at her. She backed quickly through the doorway she had seen. Turning, she spotted carved stone steps leading down below. As she started down, she heard somebody say, "Now. Pull!"

La Ombra tripped, then tumbled head first down the unforgiving, jagged stairs. The dogs rushed after her, past Lola and Burt, as she fell, thudding lower and lower into the black abyss.

CHAPTER TEN

Emerging from the cave, they pulled on their pants and agreed that the idea of taking the Bentley was a bad idea because it could be easily traced. Passing the two corpses beside it, Bert warned, "Don't look at Urrutia."

"He was such a wonderful friend," Lola said sadly.

Both of them ran down to the two lane highway.

"Where do we go now?" Burt wondered. "Bobby's next stop could be anywhere. Maybe he went directly from here to India?"

"Maybe," Lola thought a moment. "He did mention once that the *Yuz Asaf* spoke of the earliest Christian community that Jesus passed through. I think it was called Edessa. Here in Turkey."

A truck loaded with straw approached. Lola stuck out her thumb. To Burt's amazement, the driver slowed, and stopped.

"You speak English?" Lola asked him.

"Sure," he said.

"Where is Edessa?" she asked him.

"You mean Urfa," he said. "We don't call it Edessa anymore."

"Can you take us there?"

"Part way." The driver smiled at her, then spotted Burt. He shrugged in disappointment. "Just be careful of my watermelons," he said.

Lola climbed up over the rails into the bed and Burt quickly joined her. They saw it was full of straw to protect a load of green striped alligator melons.

"You sure about this Edessa, Urfa, whatever?" Burt asked.

"No, you have a better idea?"

"At least we're putting miles between us and that killer."

"You think she's dead?"

"If she didn't break her neck, I hope the dogs ate her."

As the truck got underway, Lola sat down in the straw and stared at the black, sulfurous mud caked on her jeans and tennis shoes, staining her shirt and arms. "I stink," she wrinkled her nose.

Burt looked at himself and realized he was a mess too. "We look like bums. But maybe that's okay. Maybe that's why the driver took pity on us."

"Not us," Lola smiled impishly at him. "Me. He liked me." Closing her eyes, she hugged a watermelon and stretched out on the straw and after a while, fell asleep.

As she drifted off, Burt studied her and said softly to himself, "Yeah, he liked you."

CHAPTER ELEVEN

Opening her eyes, *La Ombra* could see nothing. It was black. The side of her face ached. Somebody was moaning. Reaching out in the darkness, she found a dog's snout between her thighs. The dog lay on top of her, still alive. She jammed the gun she yet held into the beast's mouth and pulled the trigger.

In the blinding flash, she threw off the beast and struggled to her feet. A searing pain jolted her and she realized blood, her blood, was running down from her cheek. Momentarily, she recalled her vain attempt to stop from falling down the stairs, the dogs ripping at her face with their teeth as she tumbled. How far had she fallen? From her repeated head over heels crashing against the steps, her arms, chest, legs and back had been deeply bruised. Every part of her was on fire, throbbing with a hurt so deep she could not move. She took a deep breath and forced herself to think. So, the pigeons had set a clever trap for her. And with the lucky distraction of the dogs, it had worked. This time.

Shakily, *La Ombra* put a hand on a higher step and pushed herself up. Standing, legs trembling, the pain increased and she blacked out, stopping falling backwards only by clutching the side of the tunnel. Again, she fought off the dizziness, then in contempt kicked away several of the dogs' corpses, sending them thumping down the steep stairs. She thought of the cigarette lighter. But checking her pockets, realized it was gone. Lost in her fall. Beginning a long, painful climb, she blindly took step by step upward, stumbling and tripping, painfully working higher, finally gaining the top of the staircase.

Weaving unsteadily at the top of the stairs, she remembered seeing the woman use her cell phone's light. And wondered why she had not thought of her own. But searching again, found it too was gone. Probably lying somewhere at the bottom of the dank stairs.

Hugging the damp walls for what seemed like an eternity, the assassin felt her way back toward the entrance of the cave. She had no idea how long that took. It seemed like hours.

When she emerged from the mouth of Mithra's temple, she saw to her confusion blinking blue lights below. It took her a long moment to realize that it was nighttime and policemen were surrounding the bodies of Urrutia and the chauffeur yet in the *burqa* as ambulance drivers loaded them onto gurneys.

She slipped past the lights, keeping in the shadows of the hill, then worked her way out of the illuminated area. Creeping around the temple to the rear of the hill, *La Ombra* found Major Danby's Camry exactly where she had left it. No one had checked back here yet.

Slipping quickly inside, she realized that mercifully she had left the keys in the ignition. Starting up the Toyota, she eased down the back road and regained the highway at a spot far enough away from the police commotion. As *La Ombra* drove, she switched on the overhead light and checked her face in the rear view. A cur had ripped open her cheek, tearing a deep gash from her ear to nose. The deep wound would require careful cleansing, then stitches, followed by a shot of antibiotics. She reminded herself that when she could she should also inoculate herself against rabies.

After about five miles, having not passed a car, she spotted a sign in the headlights that depicted a picnic table. Turning off the highway, Delicata pulled to a stop in a copse of large overhanging sycamores. She checked and saw that there was no one around. No tents, campers or cars.

La Ombra retrieved the emergency kit she always carried from inside her luggage she had retrieved at a locker she maintained in the *Fiumicino* airport. Stepping out, she placed it on the hood and took out a battery-operated, lighted mirror from inside the kit. In its light, she carefully examined her cheek. It was worse than she thought. She could see her cheekbone, teeth and gums inside the open gash. This was going to leave a scar. A bad one. Plastic surgery would be needed.

As always when she had been hurt before, she refused to take pain killers. Trying not to pass out from the pain, *La Ombra,* as she worked the wound and began to sew it, repeatedly recited her favorite prayer. "Glory be to the Father, Son and Holy Spirit. As it was in the beginning, is now, and ever shall be, world without end. Amen."

CHAPTER TWELVE

Illuminated in the banks of portable floodlights used at crime scenes, set up directly below the mouth of Mithra's temple, Spanish Interpol Inspector Ruben Givas, a thin man with very long fingers, leaned against the fender of the Bentley limousine and watched the two bodies being loaded into a waiting ambulance. No need for paramedics to work on them. One had been identified from the contents of his wallet as Father Martin Urrutia, a citizen of Spain, and *professore* teaching at the American College in Rome. Urrutia's Spanish nationality was why Givas had been called away from vacationing on the nearby island of Crete.

On initial examination, Inspector Givas had ascertained that Father Urrutia had been shot twice, once in the mouth, another in the temple. Two well-spaced wounds, the mark of an expert. The other murdered man bore similar, well-placed wounds. He was strangely dressed in a Muslim woman's *burqa* and had no identification on him. Whoever killed him, had taken his wallet and all his papers and credit cards. Hopefully, the killer would use them. It would help track him. But it was doubtful such a pro would do something so stupid.

Turkish Police Chief Taso Surhay, also an officer in Interpol, strode back from supervising the loading of the bodies. "There is a report this car was stolen. Once, we think, driven by the dead man in the burqa. He is, or was, a chauffeur. But obviously he is not wearing his uniform now."

"Strange. Whose Bentley is it?"

"Ahmet Bendt's. Regional Governor here. I have a call into him now. Perhaps, we'll see what was going on."

Givas said, "These murders look like professional jobs."

"Executions. Without a doubt. I received a report that earlier today a killer dressed as a nun executed a priest in the Rome train station. They later found her habit in a bathroom. One of the officers remembered a priest had come out of that bathroom. He thinks now she changed in there."

"And you think this is connected? Rome is quite a distance from here."

"I am only picking at straws. I received a report from Interpol headquarters in Lyon, France. It seems that two fugitives fled that train station. One was shot in the head by this same assassin." Surhay unfolded two faxed photos. "They've been identified as an American policeman named Burt Powell and an Italian student, Lola Constantino."

"A cop? Shot? What was he doing there in Rome anyway?"

"A mystery we shall soon solve," Police Chief Surhay, who had the broad face and thick body of a wrestler, said, "I 've already placed them on our Red Notice. Something will turn up."

Givas nodded. The Red Notice would go out to all of the one hundred and eighty-six member countries of Interpol and be posted on the Wanted boards in each office.Givas belched. "Pardon me," he apologized.

"Indigestion, perhaps, *Inspectore?*" Surhay asked.

"On Crete, I believe I made the mistake of eating Turkish sheep balls."

"*Koc yumurtasi?* Our lamb testicles are delicious."

"Normally, I love testicles of calves, lambs, roosters, ducks and turkeys. And I have a weakness for *huevos de toro,* or 'bull's eggs'. But these Turkish ones tasted like offal." Givas farted loudly.

"By offal, you mean crap?" Surhay looked insulted. "I think, Inspector Givas, you must have eaten Greek sheep balls."

CHAPTER THIRTEEN

At sunset, the driver of the watermelon truck pulled to the side of the road and spread his prayer rug on the dirt shoulder. He faced Mecca in the east and began his evening prayers, bowing and praising Allah. Burt was asleep, but Lola saw there were police lights ahead on the highway, with uniformed officers stopping every car.

She shook Burt. "We have to get off."

He instantly awakened and looking ahead, understood what was happening. Swinging over the truck's railing, they both dropped silently onto the side of the highway, leaving the driver who, unaware, continued his prayers.

"Do you think they're looking for us?" Lola whispered as she bent low and ran with Burt into a drainage ditch that was parallel to the road.

"Maybe."

"They would have found the bodies by now. Maybe they're looking for us."

"Maybe."

"Is that all you can say? You're a policeman, you should know these things."

"You're right. They're looking for us. We've got to get around the roadblock. Keep down."

They moved cautiously along in the cover of the ditch. Approaching the road block bathed in bright, portable lights on metal trees, Burt pulled Lola down and flattening themselves crawled forward on their stomachs.

Lola said, "Look, our watermelon truck is driving up."

The driver rolled down his window and spoke to a uniformed cop who was showing photocopies with faces on them. At seeing them, he grew animated, gesturing to the back of his truck.

"He gave us up!" Lola whispered as they watched the scene.

As Turkish police swarmed the bed, guns drawn, Burt said, "Time to go fast."

Jumping up, and hunkering low, they duck walked along the ditch. When they were in the dark, out of the range of the floodlights, they veered off away from the highway into a ravine.

"They'll spread out and search for us, won't they?" Lola hissed, running behind Burt.

"Probably."

"What we need is a miracle. If only I had a holy relic to help us get away."

"You believe in those things?" They were keeping low, ducking down as police spread out behind them, searching on the highway.

"Absolutely. Once I even prayed to the Holy Sponge."

"What?"

"It was in the church of St. Anna in Naples. Roman soldiers used the sponge to offer Jesus wine on the cross, remember?"

"It still exists?"

"There are two sponges actually. The Archbishop of Toulouse has one and the Cardinal in Los Angeles another."

"How could there be more than one?"

"It's a mystery."

"Did your prayer work?"

"No, I got a D- on my test."

"So much for the sponge."

"But you haven't heard anything yet. I once prayed to the Holy Umbilical Cord?"

"Get out of here."

"Seriously. I wanted a new dress. It didn't work either. So I thought about praying to the Hair of Jesus. That's in Rome, I think."

"Mind boggling."

"I haven't even begun. There are tears that Jesus shed over his vision of Jerusalem destroyed."

"They have them? I mean they didn't dry up?"

"No, it was a miracle. The tears are preserved in a glass vial in Bonn, Germany."

"Lots of holy relics. Something for every occasion." "Wait, I know another. The Milk Teeth that fell out of the infant Jesus."

"You believe this stuff?"

"*Certo,* millions do," Lola replied. "There's something for everybody. I'll bet you can't name a relic that does not exist."

"Okay," Burt whispered over his shoulder as they hurried forward, stumbling in the darkened ditch. "Straw from the manger where Jesus was born."

"In Barcelona. Try again."

"Um. Let's see. What about the whip that scourged Jesus?"

"Easy, that's in Jerusalem. In a gold reliquary."

"Uh, a thorn from his crown?"

"Over three thousand of them throughout the world."

"Must have been a really big crown. Okay, I'm going all out on this one. A splinter from the sign above the cross that said 'Jesus Christ, King of the Jews.'"

"In Brooklyn."

"Brooklyn? Outstanding. What haven't I thought of?"

"The nails used to crucify the two thieves. Milan and Athens," she said. "The bones of the fishes used to feed the five thousand before the Sermon on the Mount. In Athens also."

"How many fish bones are there?"

"Lots. Teensy-weensy ones."

"Any relics from the Old Testament?"

"Not so many. Israel does have a rung of Jacob's ladder. And there's sand from when Moses parted the Red Sea."

"What about the ten commandments? Anything left of them?"

"Moses smashed them, remember?"

"But God made a duplicate."

"No mention of them. Wanna hear my all-time favorite relic?"

"Do I have a choice?"

"The Holy Prepuce."

"What the hell is that?"

"Jesus's foreskin. Left over from his circumcision. Actually, there are three sacred prepuces." Lola said. "One in London, another in Venice and a third in Paris."

"Jesus must have had a big..."

"Don't blaspheme." Lola warned him.

CHAPTER FOURTEEN

As the sun rose, Burt and Lola arrived exhausted before a towering centuries-old wall surrounding an ancient city. Several mosques with their golden domes and minarets rose high into the clear sky.

They walked on a cobble stone road through an open tall iron gate. Inside an early morning bustle of merchants were arriving in pickups and donkey carts, carrying produce from their fields. Women scurried around, carrying trays of food, serving customers who were eating breakfasts of bitter coffee and walnut pastries.

They went past stalls of beef cooking over braziers. Men serving hot tea. A sign on a building in Arabic and English announced *Urfa Hamam.*

"Guess we're in Urfa," Burt said.

"I'm hungry." She checked her pockets. "I must have lost my money when I took my jeans off in that filthy temple. How much do you have?"

Burt found his wallet. "Should have got more dollars exchanged. I only have thirty Euros."

As they walked past more stalls in the central market place, the inhabitants eyed them.

"We must look like tramps," Lola said.

"Maybe first we should clean up," Burt suggested.

"Yeah, I smell like a sewer." Lola approached a veiled woman who was arranging long, red peppers on a table in her stall. "Speak English?"

She shrugged that she didn't understand.

Lola made a scrubbing motion under her arm.

The woman grinned and pointed up the street. Lola thanked her and they went up about a block to a squat building, its front covered in beautiful cerulean blue tiles with a drawing of a hot bath.

"Must be the place," Burt said.

Inside, a stout man in a white robe was sitting behind a desk, reading a morning newspaper. He looked up.

"Twelve Euros," he said.

"You take credit cards?" Lola wondered.

The man smiled. "Visa, Master Card."

"We pay with a card,' Burt whispered to Lola, "The Hand of Christ could trace us." He dug in his wallet and handed over twenty-four Euros.

The attendant gave them fresh white towels from stacks on his table. He said something in Turkish, and when receiving no response, repeated it in awkward English, pointing in two different directions. "Man, woman?"

"We're hungry too."

"Ah, *mirra* and *sillik* with the bath?"

"Whatever," Lola told him. "I could eat a horse."

"Horse?" the man asked. "You want horse?"

"No, no, just bring whatever you said," Burt handed him another five and tipped him his final Euro.

A woman attendant appeared and led Lola into one side of the baths while Burt was shown into the men's quarters by the attendant. Alone, Burt stripped off his muddied and smelly clothes and stood naked beneath a hard spray of hot water. He washed with a thick bar of lye-smelling soap and when he was finished, the attendant pointed down a long hallway. Clad only in a bath towel around his waist, Burt trundled down the passage and entered an enormous, high-domed room that housed a steaming, round pool of clear, blue water. Dropping the towel, he slipped down up to his neck.

From behind him, through an ornate wooden screen dividing the bathing areas between men and women, Burt heard someone splash down.

"Heaven," Lola sighed blissfully.

"Better?" Burt's voice echoed across the blue tiled dome ceiling.

"Burt? Is that you?"

"No, the stinky man is gone."

"Do you have company?"

"Not a soul. You?"

"I have all this entire wonderful hot water to myself. Wait, a woman just brought me breakfast."

He could hear Lola thanking her, then: "I'm eating now. Correction, I am gobbling."

Burt looked up as the male attendant wordlessly set a silver tray beside him. Thanking him, Burt snaked a wet hand out of the water and picked up a cup of strong coffee. It was thick, hot, bitter and delicious.

Lola said with her usual directness, "Father Bobby told me you had a wife. But she died."

Burt paused, reluctant to talk about her. "Francie. She died last year. Of leukemia."

"I am sorry. Do you have a woman now?"

"You ask a lot of questions."

"I come from the streets. We have no place for nice talk. Well, do you?"

"Angie. She's my boss."

"Another cop?! Is she nice to you?"

"Better than I deserve."

"Do you love her?"

"She's a good woman."

"But you don't *love* her."

"As the song goes, 'I need her more than want her.'"

"Ah, that is sad."

"It's enough."

"For her too?"

"She knows it's all I got."

"Maybe you have more but don't know it."

He was quiet a moment. "You were in love with Bobby, weren't you?"

"It shows, huh?"

"Yeah, it shows."

"I loved him but not the way you think, not as a man. Anyway, with his vow of celibacy he could not love me back."

There was a long silence with only the sound of the water in the pools lapping at the edges. Then Lola said, "You think I am in love with you because you look like Bobby?"

"If you are, you're confused. I'm nothing like him. Nothing at all. He was a good man."

"And you are *violente*. I grew up around your kind. I do not love you. But instead of love, I will trust you. That trust will be our bond. To prove it, I will show you how much I trust you. I carry a secret that if it was revealed, I would be killed."

"You shouldn't reveal secrets, Lola. Keep it to yourself. I don't want to know something like that."

"Do this for Bobby. He knew my secret. And I trusted him."

He thought for a moment. "Alright," he said."Are you still alone over there?"

"No one else is here."

"If, while I am talking should someone enter, you must tell me immediately so I can stop. I am very afraid for anyone else to know my secret."

"Alright."

She said, "My name is not Lola Constantino. I was given that after I testified in court against the *lazzarini,* the street mafia in Napoli. The extortionists who control the shopkeepers. The drug dealers who run the slums and *piazzas* whose fountains are empty of water, drained and littered instead with used syringes and needles."

There was silence then she continued, "I am Carla Contini, a member of the dreaded and murderous Contini family who controls all business between Forza and Nola streets in Naples. Seven blocks. When I betrayed them and brought them to justice, I became in my family's eyes a whore, a worthless traitor, giving testimony against them, turning on them, doing something that is never done, something considered *infame.* I have a death sentence on my head. During the trial, they tried to execute me twice. Once when I arrived for court, guarded by the *Squadra Mobile,* the avenue before the courthouse they riddled the building with bullets from their machine pistols."

"And the other time?"

"A car bomb meant for me took instead the life of the Prosecutor who had to be replaced."

"And you put them all away? Your whole family?"

"My two brothers, four cousins, father, mother, grandmother and grandfather. All were found guilty in the high court and sentenced to life without parole. You want to know why I did that? I betrayed them all because they had my husband, Vincenzo, murdered. A good man, a fisherman by trade, who had his own fish shop on the beach. When he refused to pay their monthly *pizzo,* they killed him out of greed, as an example, as a warning, that no one, not even family was immune from their power. So, I took my revenge."

"So let me guess. Then you were hidden away in a Witness Protection Program, or whatever you call it in Italy. And everything about you got changed. Your identity gone, you got a new name too."

"*Certo.* And it was your brother, Father Bobby who helped me. He got me enrolled on a scholarship into the University at Turin. And kept my secret. Made me feel safe, and showed me that I had a future."

Burt whistled softly. "Carla Contini. Glad to meet you."

"My name is Lola, Burt."

"Lola Constantino. I think you are wrong."

"Wrong? About what?"

"I think Bobby not only trusted but loved you too."

Two men, both naked, clutching towels, slipped into the pool opposite him. "I've got company now," Burt whispered to Lola.

The younger man stared rudely at Burt.

Burt asked, "Is there a problem?"

Realizing his mistake, the man blushed, "Forgive me for my offense, sir. I am Benopo, Mayor of Urfa. It's just that you startled me. I mean, you look exactly like someone I know."

Lola, overhearing that, shouted from the other side of the screen, "Does he look like a priest? Was it Father Bobby Powell?"

Mayor Benopo lifted his face to the divider and replied, "Why, yes, yes, it was him. It was Father Bobby. Do you know him?"

CHAPTER FIFTEEN

Burt and Lola climbed out of their pools and hurried into their respective locker rooms. Inside his, Burt found his Monaco t-shirt, his own linen slacks, socks, even shoes, all cleaned, spic and span, not a trace of mud, neatly folded on a bench. Lola, toweling her hair, saw that her jeans, thin white blouse, bra, panties, and socks had also been washed and pressed.

Outside on the street, Benopo the Mayor, now dressed in a traditional white *dishdasha* and skull cap, was waiting with the other bather, chatting with several shopkeepers. When Burt and Lola came out of the baths, he said, "As I said, I am Benopo. This man is Imam Cavusoglu. He must leave to sing morning prayer at the mosque. He will meet us later. Come, I'll show you Urfa."

Cavusoglu bowed and departed and they strolled through the cool morning air, looking at the bazaar's wares, feeling clean, happy and well fed. More farmers in traditional Arabic dress, women in scarves, were arriving in donkey drawn wagons loaded with peaches, tomatoes and thin red peppers in baskets.

"That is the *isot* red pepper which we are famous for." Benopo explained, picking up a few from a basket. "In 1920, when the French conquered Urfa and destroyed the *isot* fields, we formed a resistance and kicked them out." He laughed as they strode down the dusty lane. "No one messes with our hot peppers."

Lola asked, "I'm curious as to why you speak English?"

"Urfa, with its eight bath houses, and quaint architecture is a tourist destination," Benopo explained. "Vacationers from the modern city of Istanbul escape here. As do travelers from Europe. Because it is cheap, we regularly receive visitors from the many American soldiers from Iraq who are on leave. Also, tourists from England, Scotland, Ireland, Norway, New Zealand, Australia and Canada come here."

Several of the heavy wooden doors in the houses' walls they were passing stood open, revealing inside the traditional Middle Eastern courtyards, their fountains bubbling with fresh water. As they rounded a corner, a giant dome rose before them. It was startling to see such a grand structure amid the lowly stalls and walled homes. At its center was a high minaret, six stories high.

"This is *Ulu Cami*, our Mosque," Benopo explained. "It was once the Church of the Holy Apostles."

"Wasn't this where the *Mandylion* was kept?" Lola asked.

"Ah, yes, you refer to the Arabic name for the Holy Shroud," Benopo replied. "Yes, the cloth remained here, actually above that main doorway until the Crusaders stole it in 1211. Then they took it to France."

A chanter, on top of the minaret tower above the *Ulu Cami* began to sing, calling everyone to prayer.

"Ah, here is my home." Benopo opened a white gate in a wall. "I must go pray. You will be comfortable here until I return. My wife will look after you."

After a few words of introduction by Benopo, Burt and Lola were welcomed into the compound by Hana, the mayor's wife. Pretty, dressed in a long white robe, her hair covered with a fashionable, bright blue Hermes scarf, Hana spoke English well, politely bringing them glasses of *menengic kahvesi,* a coffee-like drink.

Mayor Benopo smilingly closed the gate. But he did not go to the mosque to pray. In the baths, he had not only recognized Burt's resemblance to the priest who had come here, but as a fugitive wanted by Interpol. Striding forcefully through the village, ignoring the morning's greetings from citizens to their Mayor, Benopo headed to the cement stairs leading to the new modern street that fronted the two tourist hotels above. He entered the hotel called *Dedeman,* a pink plastered, three story building, and the only place in town that served liquor.

Inside, quickly crossing its modern lobby, he opened a back door to his mayoral offices. His secretary, Zisa, had already gone to prayer. But that did not matter. This task he could do himself. In his office, Benopo stood before his bulletin board and carefully checked the photos he had received yesterday by fax. This man and woman, Burt Powell and Lola Constantino, were wanted for questioning concerning a shooting at the Rome train station. The Interpol and Turkish police had also been notified and put out their own dragnet. Benopo studied the photos to make absolutely sure before calling. Yes, there was no doubt. It was them.

Seating himself behind his desk, the Mayor of Urfa did his duty and dialed the local police station in the larger nearby town of *Gaziantep*.

***

It was pleasant in the shade of the courtyard beneath the hibiscus trees where they sat. A fountain gurgled and splashed down into its little pond.

Lola tasted her drink and said, "Like Kahlua, without the liquor."

"Ah," Hana sighed. "I am Muslim but when I was in the States, I cheated sometimes. I have a weakness for beer."

"You were educated there?" Burt was interested.

"Suffolk University in Boston, graduated with a B.A. in Economics."

"If you don't mind my asking, what are you doing here?" Lola wanted to know.

"This is where I was born and raised. I joined my husband, who is also Kurdish. Together, we are trying to grow businesses in this part of Turkey."

The white door in the wall opened and Imam Cavusoglu who they had already met, led a gray-haired blind man into the garden. He tenderly guided the old man to the small table and settled him gently into a chair next to them.

"I have finished the prayers," he said, "And Mayor Benopo has told me you would appreciate hearing anything we can tell you about Father Bobby." He nodded to the old man. "It is why I brought Haijar."

The blind man bowed with a slow, quiet dignity. "For years, I was a professor of religious history at the University of Istanbul. After losing my sight through diabetes, I retired."

"Benopo said you are Father Bobby's brother?" Cavusoglu inquired of Burt.

"Yes, and this is Lola, Father Bobby's colleague from Turin University."

The old man, hearing that said, "Why are you trying to find him?"

Lola shot a quick at Burt. "He's dead. Somebody killed him."

"A terrible evil," Haijar moaned. "He was a light in this world. I will pray for him. What do you want to know about his visit here?"

"Anything you can recall," Burt said.

The blind teacher lifted his rheumy eyes to the morning sky as if seeing some invisible truth there. "I remember that Father Bobby was most interested in a document that he had discovered called the *Yuz Asaf*. I have never seen it but knew of it. He told me he had hidden it and memorized its contents. It relates the history of King Abgar of Edessa, ruler of this very city, now called Urfa."

The white gate in the wall burst open and Mayor Benopo, out of breath, stumbled inside.

The Imam turned, studying him a moment. "You missed prayer."

"I, uh, had business," Benopo said, mysteriously. He seemed nervous and avoided looking at Burt and Lola.

The Imam's gaze lingered on him. "Business." He said derisively, "It is always business."

Benopo sat down meekly at the table in the fifth chair and said nothing. But he kept nervously crossing and re-crossing his legs and watching the gate in the wall.

"Please continue, Haijar," Burt urged.

The old historian thought a moment, then said, "The *Yuz Asaf*, was written in 33 A.D. It recorded that Jesus, peace be upon him, arrived here in Urfa, then called Edessa, in poor health. And that he was accompanied by the Apostle Thomas, Mary Magdalen and his mother, Mary. It also stated that *Issa,* which is our Arabic name for him, was crippled after being nailed to a cross. He used a staff to walk. After several years here, Jesus, peace be upon him, grew well enough to travel. And moved on."

Burt said, "Is this document reliable?"

Haijar said. "The *Yuz Asaf* is corroborated by a total of twenty-one other historical writings I have read that bear witness to this same history, namely, that Jesus, peace be upon him, survived the cross and came here."

"Tell them the rest, master," Imam Cavusoglu, who had remained quietly in the background, now requested.

"After Jesus left from here, he went with his mother, Mary, his wife, Mary Magdalen and the apostle St. Thomas north into India. There, he resided in the Himalayan mountains as a guest of King Gondophares. In a document written in 60 A.D. that I have seen, called the *Bhavisyat Mahapuranas,* which is preserved in a London Museum, the King's scribe relates in great detail how Jesus, his mother, and Mary Magdalen lived there in the palace of King Gondophares for many years."

"We know also that Jesus went to India because the Jewish tribe of *Bnei Menash* was there. He was safe there from his enemies. It is the tribe of Mary, his mother. Even to this day, the *Bnei Menash* live there in the *Pir Panjal* mountains which are in the Western Himalayas. As a matter of fact, as we speak, the state of Israel is attempting to bring the entire tribe home. You can read about it on Google. My grandson found the article for me."

Imam Cavusoglu sighed. "With the Internet, it is a small world today."

Outside the wall, there was the sound of a police siren approaching.

"Ah, they are here," Benopo rose.

Hana stared suspiciously at her husband. "What did you do?"

"My duty. These two are fugitives. I reported them."

"They are strangers who we must protect," the Imam murmured. "If you would come to prayer more often, perhaps you would know that it is our duty as Muslims to shelter and assist travelers."

The siren died as it halted right outside the wall.

CHAPTER SIXTEEN

Haijar sat perfectly still, listening to the shouts from the policemen outside, ordering them to open the gate. "Those men are from *Gaziantep*," he whispered to Imam Cavusoglu. "I recognize their voices. Do not let them in."

One of the policemen banged loudly on the gate.

"Where did Bobby go next?" Burt asked Haijar.

"I know the answer to that," Hana, who was standing nearby, said, "Father Bobby sent emails to two Universities in India, requesting information on Jesus. He said someone named Kali agreed to meet him at an ancient Hindu temple in New Delhi."

"Yes," Haijar confirmed it. "He said the man was from a university, named Kali."

Burt said, "What was the temple?"

They both tried to remember.

Hana finally said, "He only mentioned it was where St. Thomas had once preached."

"Open up." a policeman outside commanded. "Mayor Benopo. We can hear you inside. What is going on?"

"I forbid you to open the gate," the Imam scolded Benopo. "You will not help them. That is your penance for missing prayer."

Lola said to Burt. "We have to get to Delhi."

Burt took out his wallet and slapped down his Visa card on the table. "If I use a credit card, that assassin will follow us so we have to cover our tracks." Turning to Hana, he asked, "Can you purchase twenty flight tickets to different destinations?"

"To where?"

"Anywhere. It doesn't matter. Just make sure two tickets go to New Delhi."

"You'll have to take a plane from *Esenboga* International in Ankara to New Delhi," Haijar said.

Clutching Burt's credit card, Hana ran into her house. "I'll make the purchases and print out your e-tickets."

The policemen threw their shoulders against the gate to break it down.

"Be ready to go," Imam Cavusoglu announced to Burt and Lola.

Lola crossed to Haijar and kissed his cheek. "Thank you for everything. You're great."

"If only my wife would realize that," Haijar joked.

"Benopo," Imam Cavusoglu commanded. "Now, give our guests that motorbike of yours."

"My bike? I'll be arrested for helping them." Benopo objected. But seeing the fierce look on his Imam's face, he furtively guided Lola and Burt inside the house.

Haijar, hearing the policemen throw themselves on the gate, calmly suggested to Imam Cavusoglu, "Perhaps you should let them in now before they destroy something."

"Good idea. And before I answer any of their questions, I will find out if these two policemen are being good, observant Muslims." Walking to the gate, he unlocked and flung it open.

CHAPTER SEVENTEEN

After she inserted the curved needle in a final stitch into the bloody flap of skin and muscle on her face, she tied off the suture. With the sky growing light, revealing a rushing muddy river below where she had parked the Toyota, *La Ombra* washed her face and hands with alcohol and antiseptic sheets that she kept in her medical kit for just this purpose. Changing out of the chauffeur's uniform, Delicata opened her suitcase to carefully choose her next deception.

Selecting a gray wig, she fitted it on her head, then next took out a widow's dress from its dry cleaner's plastic bag. Pulling it on, she covered her swollen and badly scarred face with a black veil, then tied it beneath her chin to hide the grievous wound. Studying herself in the lighted mirror, still balanced on the Toyota's hood, she checked her appearance and satisfied at her transformation, packed her things to go.

Inwardly, she seethed. Her beauty had been ruined by these two pigeons who refused to die. They would pay. Their deaths would be slow and horrible.

Her spare cell she always kept on hand buzzed.

Delicata reached inside her old woman's black dress pocket and checked the readout. It was from her hired nerds in Lausanne, Switzerland, a company called International Database, that constantly fed her information about everything from weather to maps to tracking phone calls and credit card purchases on her prey. Of course, none of them knew what she did.

A secure read-out appeared from 'Captain Kangaroo', their corny code name.

Delicata pushed the receive button and a message texted on her screen. "Purchaser, Mr. Burt Powell, Visa xxx-xxxx-xxxxxxx, flight 1304, Athens to Madrid."

She stared at the screen, not understanding. One of her pigeons had bought a ticket from Athens? It didn't make sense.

Then another text replaced the first. "Purchased by Burt Powell, Visa, xxx-xxxxx-xxxx, flight 212, American Airlines Ankara to Denver."

Something was wrong here.

In short order, more conflicting data rolled across the cell phone's screen, listing ETDs from Cairo, Jerusalem, and ETAs in Madrid, Rome, Budapest, Amsterdam.

Now, *La Ombra* smiled. These two were better than she thought. But they could not know what she did. She paused the latest text read out and scrolled back, freezing it at one that had caught her eye. A flight to New Delhi. Lufthansa Airlines, one way, flight 113/1070, Ankara to Indira Gandhi Airport, New Delhi. Departure 1:30 pm. Arrival 5:10 A.M. Flight time, 15 hours, 40 minutes."

Where Powell's brother, the priest, had last gone to and where she had dispatched him. They were now retracing his steps. It had to be.

Sliding inside Major Danby's Toyota, *La Ombra* drove up onto the two lane highway and turning in the opposite direction from where she had come from Incirlik airport, she headed north toward Ankara. Checking herself in the rear view, she was at least satisfied to see an elderly hag stare back at her. The costume and greyish face make-up played nicely.

La Ombra calculated it would take three hours to Ankara. She reminded herself that before entering that huge city, she would have to abandon the Toyota. By now, the Major's car would be reported stolen and perhaps even his body found. The Shadow withdrew her rosary beads and to fight the constant pain throbbing in her face, began to say the "Glorious Mysteries", not the "Sorrowful" or "Joyful". It would keep her mood buoyant.

CHAPTER EIGHTEEN

Burt drove Mayor Benopo's rattling Kawasaki motorbike down the dirt road out of Urfa. Lola, seated behind him, arms tight around his waist, turned and checked behind them. No one was after them. Yet. Moments before, they had driven the bike out of Mayor Benopo's garage and were now leaving a fantail of dust in their wake. Cows, chewing their cuds, watched passively from their pastures as they roared past.

Lola shouted. "How far did Benopo say it was to the train tracks?"

"Three kilometers."

"And from there to Ankara?"

"Six hours. If we catch the freight train in time."

"There," Lola cried. "I see it, up ahead. It looks old, a bunch of rusted cars."

"It doesn't look like it's stopping." Burt swung off the road and down toward the tracks. The slow moving line of cars rattled ahead of them and he sped up until the motorcycle was even with an open door.

Burt yelled, "When I get close enough, stand up on the seat and leap inside the car."

"*Porca miseria.*"

"Bloody hell, right?"

"You're learning." Lola stood, grabbed hold of his shoulders, balancing herself precariously.

"How about something stronger for the occasion." Burt egged her on.

"*Figlio di puttana!*" she screamed.

He fought to hold the small distance between them and the iron box car as it clattered along. Lola leaped head first, but landed on the metal edge of the open door, legs wriggling above the turning iron wheels below. Burt gave her butt a shove and she hauled herself inside.

Seeing she was safe, he thrust his right hand out and caught hold of the box car's door. The bike's front tire hit a rock, tossing Burt into the air. Lola grabbed hold of his arm just as the bike skidded out of control. With Lola jerking him forward, he catapulted inside and landed on top of her.

For a moment, they lay that way, intertwined, not wanting to move, too overcome by what had just happened to recognize their intimate position.

Then Burt muttered, "Thanks."

"*Prego*," she responded in a low, soft voice. Then seeing the motorcycle race driverless outward, then careen back toward the lumbering box cars, she said "Benopo's bike!"

Sticking their heads out the door, they saw the Kawasaki dramatically dive under the train's enormous wheels. A box car crushed the bike, then spat it out making it cartwheel, finally flopping unmoving into a mangled, smoking heap.

Lola asked, "Do you think Benopo can fix it?"

"It'd take a miracle."

"Serves him right. He called the cops on us."

They both scooted back deeper inside the dilapidated freight car, sitting quietly as it swayed back and forth, rocking on the tracks. Lola saw Burt close his eyes, and cross his hands on the Monaco shirt. For a long time, she stared out the open door of the freight car, seeing the flat expanse of green fields pass outside.

When she turned back to Burt, she saw that for the first time since they had met, he was sleeping. He looked vulnerable and sweet.

Lola lay down next to him and fell asleep.

CHAPTER NINETEEN

New Delhi, India
Interpol Bureau Headquarters

Inspector Rohan Jodpat, a dark, handsome young man with swept back black hair and intense eyes, was watching the BBC video of Indian Energy Minister Naik Mayang, recorded yesterday in Leal, Sudan. The ragtag refugee camp, composed mostly of women and children fleeing the Janjaweed butchers, was surrounded by a flat, treeless plain. The refugees were standing, watching Mayang, a member of Indian Parliament, as he stood on the bed of a truck, speaking out against a proposed oil pipeline deal, involving India, China and Malaysia.

"It is morally wrong for us to enter into this agreement. For the Indian government to invest in this fashion violates all our principles and even International law. This deal will bring more arms to the Sudanese government and kill more helpless people like those in Darfur."

Jodpat had met the fiery minister once and had admired his integrity. Some had compared him to the great Mahatma Gandhi.

Dressed smartly in his dark business suit, Naik continued, "While I realize India's home sources of oil are declining, and that we must find new imports, this is not the way. If we do this deal, we will profit short-term. But the world will condemn us for it and we will lose in the end..."

Without warning, the image of Naik Mayang simply shredded into rags flying into the air and a spray of blood splattering the camera lens. The cameraman dropped his camera, and in the fallen lens, he and the reporter could be seen fleeing in shock. The refugees began screaming and Sudanese soldiers randomly and stupidly fired out into the desert at nothing.

Inspector Jodpat turned off the recording. He had viewed it a half dozen times and each time had come to the same conclusion. This was the work of a hired gun, a sniper. Military, perhaps. Sudanese army. But someone really good.

Using a big, very powerful weapon, at least 50 caliber, from a long way away. The clog in the oil deal had been removed. It had been announced in this morning's edition of *The Times of India's* financial section that the Sudan pipeline, previously halted, was now going forward.

There was a knock at the door and Nevo Muzzafaro, Jodpat's assistant, entered. As usual, his tie was askew, slipped to one side and his white shirt wrinkled. He was carrying a file.

"Good morning, sir."

Inspector Jodpat stood and buttoned the jacket of his dark blue suit. "You look like you've been up all night, Nevo."

"I worked and slept here," Muzzafaro smiled.

Late last night the CIA, routinely monitoring the movement of the Janjaweed on its spy satellite, informed Indian Interpol that shortly before their Energy Minister was assassinated in Sudan, a phone call had been placed from a nearby hilltop.

"Any luck on tracking it?" Jodpat wondered.

"I learned the transmission was relayed through a Chinese Communications satellite."

"Will the Chinese release the records?"

"No, it was a military satellite and they say it involves national security. However, we may have got a break. Our Intelligence was able to determine that the call was roaming, forwarded by a land-based station into Turkey."

"Exactly where?"

"Tarsus."

Jodpat looked at his computer screen. "This bulletin came in this morning. Spanish and Turkish Interpol Bureaus are hunting two fugitives in Tarsus, Turkey. They found two murder victims there too of a Catholic priest and a chauffeur. Is there a connection?"

Jodpat punched a button and the photos of Burt Powell and Lola Constantino appeared side by side on the monitor. "These are the two fugitives."

The Assistant stared at Burt. "I think that a priest, Father Bobby Powell, who shares the last name with one of the fugitives, was here in Delhi. I believe he committed suicide by hanging himself on the Royal Gardens bridge."

"I remember," Inspector Rohan said. "It happened in the temple district. Another was murdered at that same time by someone witnesses said was dressed like a cartoon. To be precise, a Japanese anime girl." Rohan scratched his head.

"I wonder, are these different pieces of the puzzle connected? Or is it just a coincidence?"

He punched in an update request to Interpol. Reading the screen, he said, "It seems this fugitive, Mister Burt Powell is an American policeman."

"Really. More and more interesting."

"And he recently bought plane tickets to multiple destinations."

"Why would he do such a thing?"

"One destination will interest us. He purchased two to here, in New Delhi. I have his flight number. We'll put out a watch to intercept him and perhaps his traveling companion, Miss Constantino, if and when they arrive."

CHAPTER TWENTY

The continuing police investigation inside Mayor Benopo's walled house had not gone well. Despite threats to arrest the Imam, Haijar, the blind man, the wife and Benopo himself, the group remained constant in their wildly differing destinations of where the fugitives had fled.

In addition, two Interpol officers, Turkish Police Chief, Taso Surhay and Spanish Inspector Ruben Givas had arrived and joined the interrogation. But they also learned nothing new. After a while, they retreated outside the wall to confer.

"Kurdish peasants." Surhay muttered "I've seen this before. They stick together like concrete."

Then they got a break. The local police from *Gaziantep* returned, saying they had found the remains of a crushed Kawasaki along the train tracks. Surhay ordered them to phone ahead and have the train stopped and searched.

"Which way, sir?" the younger policeman asked.

"What? Wherever it's going." Surhay shouted.

"That's just it, sir." The older one who was perhaps twenty-five and had a black mustache objected. "The rail lines split at Maras and again at Malataya. From there, they go off in four, no, five different directions."

"Then cover them all," Surhay commanded.

The local police from looked at each other.

"Well, what are you waiting for?"

The officers saluted and retreated to their parked car. The Mustache, speaking in Kurdish, said, "That Interpol big shot doesn't give the orders. Our Captain must do that."

"Where is the Captain?" the younger one whispered.

The mustache checked his watch. "Milking his goats."

"We better check with him first." And he picked up the radio mike.

As Surhay and Givas walked to Surhay's Police Chief car, Givas said, "Ever since arriving in Turkey, I've been hungry. Where is there a decent place to eat around here?"

"I believe," Surhay said patiently to him, "you would enjoy some *doner* or perhaps *kavurma*. Both are barbecued kabobs of mutton and calf's liver."

Inspector Givas sighed. "All during the roadblock last night on the highway I dreamed of *fabada,* a delicious bean stew with pork that we enjoy in Spain."

"We are Muslims, here. We do not eat pork."

"Pity," Givas said. "Seven hundred years ago, we threw out all the Moors in Asturias and now we enjoy pork. Perhaps, then, some *callos?*"

"What is that?"

"Tripe. A cow's stomach."

"In Spain, you eat the stomach of a cow?"

"It is a delicacy for those who are sophisticated," Givas said. "It also cures hangovers."

"We don't drink here either. So we have no hangovers."

"What a waste. Perhaps you have heard of *gobernada,* chunks of meat, cooked with onion, garlic and white wine sauce?"

"No," Surhay said. "But if you were to open up your mind a little and try something new, like our *cig kofte,* you might learn a thing or two. But then again, the meat is seasoned with our *isot* hot peppers and would probably burn your delicate tongue."

Inspector Givas' cell phone rang. He answered it and said to Surhay, "I'd better take this. It's from Interpol Headquarters in Lyon, France."

"I know where our headquarters are," Surhay responded indignantly. "I have been there many times myself. Why are they calling you instead of me? This is my country and my jurisdiction."

"I do not know. Anyway, they asked me to hold a moment," Givas told him. "It seems the Executive Director himself is calling. By the way, he loves our tripe."

Police Chief Surhay blew out his breath and walked away a few feet, muttering to himself.

"Director," Spanish Inspector Givas said brightly. "Yes, this is Inspector Ruben Givas. Well. I am well, sir. Alright, yes, yes, I understand. I did have other plans. I was taking my children to a *futbol* game on Crete this weekend, but I will most certainly change them."

He pulled out his notebook and pen. "Yes, I have his name. Indian Interpol Chief Rohan Jodpat. In New Delhi. Yes, I most certainly understand the importance of this assignment. Thank you for thinking of me, Mister Executive Director. I will do my best."

Givas shut off the phone and placed it back inside his pocket. Surhay was staring at him.

"Oh, well," Givas said as if he just remembered Surhay was still here. "Executive Director Noble has personally ordered me to fly to New Delhi. It seems the Indian Interpol National Central Bureau Chief Rohan Jodpat there has recognized that a Father Bobby Powell is related to one of our fugitives. And he has discovered that it is where at least one of our fugitives is going next. I have been given personal orders to assist in the interception."

"None of the peasants here mentioned that the fugitives went to New Delhi," Surhay objected.

"As you said, these Kurds lie. So tell me where can I catch the nearest international flight?"

"Esenboga, in Ankara. By the way, did the Executive Director mention what I was to do?"

"He didn't say," Givas responded. "Which means, I suppose, you are to pursue the case from this end. In Turkey."

"But why did he sent you instead of me? I don't understand."

"Perhaps because you are also Chief of Police and you have other duties. As for myself, I am dedicated only to Interpol." Givas walked to the car they had both arrived in. "Of course, I will need you to take me to Esenboga."

Surhay said through clenched teeth. "Take the car. I won't need it for a while. I'll get another ride." He gestured to the two policemen who were both smoking, waiting for their Captain to call back and tell them what to do.

Swinging inside, Givas said to Surhay, "Who knows? Maybe in Delhi, I will even find a decent meal."

CHAPTER TWENTY—ONE

Esenboga Airport

Ankara

Gate 23

Initially, Inspector Ruben Givas had intended to book himself on Turkish airlines flight #1244 to New Delhi. But then, once in the main terminal, in his trained-cop habit of checking faces, he had, to his amazement, spotted the two fugitives as they passed by. For a moment, he stared disbelieving at them as they wound through the crowd in front of him. There was no doubt. It was Burt Powell and Lola Constantino. He followed as they walked toward Gate 23. The flight was already boarding.

Hurrying to board Lufthansa Airlines flight 113/1070, Burt and Lola had no way of knowing that Inspector Givas was trailing them.

"Boarding passes, please." The Lufthansa gate attendant stuck out her hand impatiently. Burt handed her their electronic tickets. She ran them through her scanner and said, "Have a nice flight."

Together, they entered the boarding chute and walked down toward the 767's open door.

Behind them, Inspector Givas bought a ticket on flight 113/1070 and handed his Interpol badge with its photo identification to the counter lady. "I am carrying my weapon," the Inspector informed her.

"They have already confirmed that at Security, Inspector. You may board."

If there had been no seat available, he had already determined that he would pull the two off the plane and arrest them here and now. But that would not reveal why they were going there. And Givas had a hunch that going to New Delhi was better. Besides, he would be following orders and gain credit in the eyes of the Executive Director. Momentarily, Givas pictured how pleased the Interpol Executive Director would be. Yes, this was the smart thing to do. The Director would reward him perhaps with a promotion, perhaps even a desk job at the Lyon headquarters itself. Anyway, where would the two go on the plane? He could watch them every second. Givas could already see the headlines. As he noted where the two were sitting and strapped himself into a seat three or four rows behind them, he actually rehearsed what he would say in the interviews with the news. Fame was on the horizon.

***

Several hours ago, *La Ombra,* having ditched the Major's Toyota, stole a black SUV from a shopping center near Islip from a woman loading her groceries. She drove the last few miles into Esenboga. Now that she had learned from the Fabrizio family's intelligence team in Lausanne, Switzerland that her pigeons had already bought their e-tickets for the Lufthansa flight 113/1070 to New Delhi, she had them buy her one on that flight as well.

Parking the SUV directly in front of the terminal in the pick-up zone, she hurried to the boarding gate and to her surprise spotted her pigeons waiting in line. She kept them carefully in view as they got on the plane. Showing her e-ticket with its boarding pass, she presented her Italian passport with its photo depicting the old woman she now was. In character, she slowly limped up the covered ramp toward the waiting jet.

Looking for her seat, *La Ombra* deliberately waddled down the aisle. She couldn't decide whether to kill her pigeons while in the air or wait until Delhi when they got off. But doing it inside the confines of the plane meant that an escape route did not readily present itself. Still, being so close to them and furious at what they had done to her, it was tempting. Even if it did violate one of her basic rules.

Settling herself in her economy class aisle seat, she was pleased that she had a direct sight line and could easily observe her quarry on the opposite side of the plane. They were sitting nine rows ahead of hers. The nerds in Lausanne had done their research. Of course, she had been forced to leave her Glock inside her check-on luggage. But she had easily evaded the metal detector with her five-inch graphite stiletto taped to the inside of her thigh. And because of her frail appearance, had been waved past the body scanner by a most agreeable young man.

A thin man with long fingers swung past her and she momentarily caught a fleeting glimpse of a shoulder holster inside his jacket with a gun tucked inside.

As he passed, their eyes locked momentarily and she forced a feeble smile. The man nodded politely and kept going further back into the plane. Was this a new complication? What was he doing here? He might be an air marshal, just doing his duty. Or…or what?

Waiting a moment, she turned and saw him take a seat a few rows behind her. A thousand questions flashed through her mind. Was he here on some sort of business that did not concern her? Perhaps it all meant nothing. Perhaps it was merely innocent circumstances. But in her line of work, Delicata Fabrizio had long survived by never believing anything was merely coincidental.

Quickly she scanned for Powell and Constantino. They did not seem aware of any threatening situation, casually talking, looking relaxed and stupid. Behaving like amateurish sitting ducks. Still she had to be sure. And there was a simple, efficient way to figure all this out.

Swiveling slowly back to the man with the gun, she waited until he turned to look out the window, then raised her phone and snapped his photo. She sent it to Lausanne.

In a few minutes, as the plane rolled toward the runway, his data identification returned.

He was Interpol Officer, Inspector Ruben Givas, from Spain.

Now she remembered something. Upon emerging from Mithra's temple, she had seen several men in suits in the portable lights. While the bodies were being loaded, they were talking to one another. And one of them was Givas. She was sure of it.

Now the question was, why was he aboard this flight? Did he know her pigeons were on board? And if he did, why hadn't he arrested them? Or was he innocently flying to New Delhi for some other reason. More and more coincidences.

A new disturbing thought intruded in her analysis of this strange situation. How much did this Interpol officer know about the Church's secret document the priest had stolen? Probably nothing, yet. But given time, he might. And what would happen after he got to New Delhi? He would interfere with her plans to kill the pigeons. She could take no chances. The Interpol cop must be eliminated and removed from the mix.

Satisfied that she had correctly sorted out the solution, she began to form an imminent plan. *La Ombra* closed her eyes and visualized precisely what she would do. Down to every last movement. This would be a long flight. Over fifteen hours. When it was night-time and the cabin was darkened, with most passengers sleeping, she would thrust her graphite, needle-nosed dagger into the cop's heart.

Upon arrival in New Delhi, she would ask the stewardess because of her infirmity to let her get first off the plane. Maybe she'd even ask for a wheelchair. That would be a nice touch. Once in the airport, with her escape options open, she would force her pigeons into some secluded spot, kill them, search them for the stolen document and complete her assignment.

The plane lifted into the sky. It was strange to return to Delhi. The place where she had first dealt with the priest but never found the document. Perhaps he had mailed it to someone. That was still a possibility. Maybe to his brother or that slut girl sitting up ahead. Maybe this was how God worked in mysterious ways. In returning here, back to the original place where it had begun, it was part of His Divine Majesty's Will.

La Ombra felt for her rosary and began to recite the five Glorious Mysteries in thanks.

CHAPTER TWENTY—TWO

Lola checked her watch. It was 4:33 am. They were nearly fifteen hours into the flight. During the night, the cabin lights had been lowered and most of the passengers dozed. Outside, the morning sky was dark yet, sprinkled with stars, a half- moon hovering in her window.

"I have to go to the bathroom," she told Burt who was awake. She unbuckled her seat belt, stood up and went toward the back of the plane.

In preparation for arrival, the attendants brightened the lights in the cabin. One of them announced they would be landing momentarily in New Delhi. Passengers began rousing themselves, waking up, gathering their things. The stewardesses swept through the rows, collecting trash, offering cold bottles of water. Burt accepted some water and swept his gaze back to the bathrooms. It had been nearly ten minutes and Lola had not returned.

An attendant stopped and told Burt, "Put your tray up, sir. Bring your seat all the way forward and fasten your seat belt. We're landing momentarily."

He did as he was told. Again, Burt checked the bathrooms. Where was she? Then he saw Lola emerge. She took her time, sauntering forward, placing one hand after another on the seat backs, steadying herself as the 767 descended down through the air. As she passed a man who was apparently asleep, with his head lolling to one side, her hip brushed against him and to her surprise, he slumped forward in his seat. Unnerved, she stared momentarily at what had appeared to be a sleeping form Now she saw the front of his shirt was covered in blood. Backing away, she found herself locking eyes with an old woman who was glaring at her.

Lola hurried forward and sat down beside Burt.

"What's wrong?" Burt asked. "I saw you jump. What happened back there?"

Lola looked petrified, unable to speak. She sputtered, "That man I was next to. He has blood on his chest. He looks dead."

"Where?" Burt spun around, checking.

She pointed.

He saw the man, with his head bent forward.

"I think I saw her."

"Saw who?"

"That *puta,* the nun, the chauffeur, whoever she is."

"The killer? On this plane? We're on the other side of the earth, Lola. Impossible."

"She's in disguise. But I tell you it is her," Lola said. "I saw her eyes. She's back there. She was looking at me. That old woman. I could see a terrible cut on her face. I know it's her. Do you believe me?"

"It's not important if I believe you. What has to happen next is as soon as we land, we have to get off the plane fast. Once they find the body, the police will cordon this off and begin interrogating everybody. And they'll arrest us."

As soon as the plane had stopped at the boarding gate, they jumped up and rushed forward to the exit.

A stewardess said, "Are you catching another flight?"

"We've only got a few minutes," Burt said.

"Then good luck."

As soon as the 787's door opened, Lola and Burt hurried into the terminal and entered a passageway toward Indian Customs and Central Excise.

"We have to go through Customs and show our passports?"

"We're not doing that."

"Then what are we doing?"

"Just stay close and when I say scoot, we scoot."

"Scoot?"

"Get the hell out of here." He pulled Lola toward the line of Customs desks where the Indian officers were sorting arriving passengers through, opening and checking their luggage on tables.

"Sir, you must get back in line for Customs," an officious Indian in khaki uniform commanded.

Burt pulled Lola to the front of the line.

"Where is your luggage?" a Royal Indian Customs officer demanded. "You have to wait your turn, sir!"

To the bureaucrat's surprise, the couple never stopped, but fled past him.

"Stop them!" the officer ordered.

Burt ignored him and yanked Lola into a trot down the stairs.

With Customs officers pursuing, they descended the stairs. At the bottom, Burt spotted two men in black suits, their identification police badges hanging from handkerchief pockets, looking for somebody.

"Cops," he identified them.

"Are they here for us?"

"Maybe."

"There you go again, maybe, maybe. Maybe they're here for her!"

As they neared the bottom of the stairwell, the two policeman started toward them. Behind, three Customs Officials were yelling at them to halt. An enormous baggage cart was just passing, pushed by two baggage handlers. Running at it, Burt shoved the tall pile of suitcases over, scattering luggage everywhere. The cops and Customs officials tripped and were delayed just moments as Burt and Lola dove into the teeming mass of people.

Spotting the glass doors that opened out onto the street. Burt, with Lola in tow, rammed through the crowded check in lines and with a final lurch, exited the front of the Lufthansa terminal. Spotting a line of motorbike rickshaws, ready for hire, Burt picked the closest one and pushed Lola inside. The taxi driver at the head of the line was a brown, skinny, shirtless young man in tattered shorts. They quickly climbed inside and Burt told him, "Go."

"Go to where?"

"Anywhere. We're tourists. Take us around. We're in a hurry."

A policeman and several Custom officials burst through the sliding doors, looking around.

Burt ducked down inside the cab. "Hurry up, we only have an hour before we catch another plane."

"I will give you a very fast, quick and best tour ever!" the Indian laughed in his lilting tongue. "Very well. Hang on. You are about to see New Delhi!"

As they shot off, Lola said, "You know we don't have any money."

"Least of our problems."

***

La Ombra had watched her pigeons depart from the plane. Acting the part of a toddling old woman, she excused her way forward. It wasn't easy, what with so many bodies pressed so tightly together, waiting to get off. But the stewardess, true to her word, made a path for Delicata and brought her to the front door, ahead of the pressing crowd of passengers waiting to de-board.

Once off the plane, she declined the waiting wheel chair and like a re-born oldster, raced through Customs. In the commotion and confusion as the fugitives ahead of her avoided the Customs officers and the pursuing two plainclothes policemen, *La Ombra* dodged the spilled baggage cart and through the glass windows, spotted her pigeons fleeing. They were headed to a line of motorized rickshaws, parked waiting in line at the curb.

Behind her, there was more shouting and arriving airport police began blowing whistles. For a moment, she wondered if it possible that they were after her? As she neared the front sliding doors, Indian street cops in khaki tan, clutching rubber clubs rushed in, joining with the plainclothes and the Customs officials.

"No one is allowed to leave the terminal!" a tan Captain shouted.

La Ombra slowed, thinking. Apparently they had not seen her pigeons escape outside. She hunched over like an old crone and limped toward a junior cop, barring the doorway.

She said, "I forgot my medicine or I will go into convulsions. It is outside in my car. Can you get it for me? I know no one can leave. I know the law."

The cop looked around, then said, "Not you, mama. You may go."

CHAPTER TWENTY—THREE

The cabbie launched out into traffic, perilously coming within inches of a smoke belching truck. He wove through stopped traffic, horns honking at them. The cacophony was deafening as inside their *tuk-tuk*, Burt yelled to Lola, "Where was Bobby killed?"

"Some Hindu temple."

"There must be a lot of them. How are we going to find out which one?"

"I remember Hana said Bobby told her it was where St. Thomas preached." Lola opened her iphone and logged onto the Internet, then typed in "St. Thomas, India."

There were several lengthy articles about the Apostle's historical exploits, including one from Wikipedia, but nothing concerning a temple. Scrolling down, she found an entry for "Thomas the Apostle in Delhi. "

"It says here the apostle preached at the *Nili Chhatri.*"

Burt stared at the photo, then thrust the cell up to the driver. "Where's this?" he asked.

He glanced back at it. "In the Old Section."

"Take us there."

The cabbie swiftly turned off the boulevard and headed in a new direction. Swinging into a narrower, winding section of alleys and lanes, he whizzed past shoppers checking out merchandise in merchants' stalls and bazaars.

"This is *Chandi Chowk* market place." The driver shouted over his shoulder. "Very famous. Bargains. Most enjoyable."

They rolled past what he next announced was "the ancient three kilometers long, thirty meters high, most famous red sandstone fort, built by the brothers who founded Delhi.

"At night, the department of tourism holds a light show. Very impressive. Very enjoyable."

To Burt and Lola's irritation, he continued explaining that the "Elephant gate" they were passing held the *Fatehpuri* mosque, erected by the wives of the Emperor Shah Jahan.

"He's giving us the grand tour," Lola objected.

"Well, I did tell him we were tourists," Burt said.

Without warning, the driver stopped the rickshaw, opened his arms expansively and proclaimed, "And there is the *Nili Chhatri*. Temple you seek."

As they alighted and looked up at the enormous stone face rising before them with its rain-worn facade replete with carved bare-breasted goddesses, writhing and copulating in sexually acrobatic positions, the cabbie said, "This temple celebrates fertility, life."

Lola grinned, "I've never seen any of our saints depicted doing this."

"Might make a lot of converts." Burt tried not to smile as they walked up the steps into the temple.

Inside the great structure, it was cooler. Vines grew along the walls. Beggars, the infirm, some with horrible deformities in their hands, feet, others stricken with dissolving faces caused by leprosy, stubs of arms extended, asked for money.

Lola handed out a few coins to them.

One beggar, who appeared totally healthy, yelled at her, "If you want to be reincarnated, you must be generous."

"Believe me," Lola said, "Once here is enough, buddy."

Burt said, "You don't be careful, you could return as a cow."

"Long as it's a sacred one."

They scanned the temple, then studied the tight, twisting little alley below. "You think this is where Bobby met that guy Kali?"

There was a ramshackle wooden hut on the corner that housed public restrooms, from which they could smell the stench. Across the street, produce sellers displayed limes, oranges, lemons in baskets.

"What are we looking for?" Lola asked.

"I don't know. Anything. Nothing. Something out of the ordinary."

"It's probably a waste of time even coming here."

"Somebody must have seen something," Burt said. "Maybe one of these shopkeepers." He turned around. On the opposite corner stood a dilapidated police station, its windows broken and taped. A stained copper sign on its front noted "Vespery Police Station. Built November 13, 1902."

"Bingo! Cops had to know about Bobby's murder." Burt said.

They hurried down. In front of the station was a community billboard with several notices tacked to it. One was a paper- announcing that the station was slated for destruction in a month. Next to it, a drawing showed the new modern facility that would be erected in its place.

Burt turned toward the door, but Lola stopped him.

"You can't go in there." she hissed. "The cops are after us."

"Wait outside," he told her. "They're looking for two, not one."

He entered the rundown lobby of the station, its scarred chest-high front counter holding only a dusty black rotary telephone. The smell in here was years of overwhelming body odor.

Burt tapped a little bell. In a moment, an obese Indian cop in khakis, neck creased in rolls of fat, stuck his head out from the back.

"We have no tourism information." he said.

"I'm a police officer from the United States." Burt flashed his badge. "I'm looking for information about a priest who was murdered here about a month ago."

The officer reluctantly hitched up his pants and forced himself to waddle behind the counter. He opened several squeaking drawers, pulled out a pile of notices and slapped them down on the counter. "You may look through them. But you are not allowed to take them."

"What are they?"

"Why my file of past crimes committed in this section."

Leafing quickly through the pile, Burt noted that most concerned minor thefts, motor accidents and drunkenness. Then he found himself staring at a dead Indian in a white tunic, lying in the street, a pool of black blood beneath his head.

"Who's this?" he asked.

The policeman bent close and said, "We are still investigating it."

"Was his name Kali?"

"I do not know. I cannot remember every victim."

Burt stared at the photo. Was this the man named Kali that Bobby was meeting here?

"When was he killed?"

The Indian cop glanced at the photo. "I believe approximately a month ago now."

Quickly, Burt deduced it was within the time frame of Bobby's murder. So it was possible this man might have met him. It also meant his brother's murder could be connected.

"Were there any witnesses to this murder?"

"No one willing to say so. But one mentioned the assassin was a young woman dressed like a demon!"

"A demon?"

"Wearing a mask, in promiscuous clothing."

"Do you have any leads on this demon?"

"That is not my job," the Indian policeman said. "You would have to speak to our homicide division about that."

Burt thought a moment. "The victim had no papers on him? Nothing to show who he was?"

Tired of these questions, exhaling loudly in frustration, the officer rudely snatched the paper that Burt held, turned it over and slapped it down. "There!" he said, as if that solved this inquiry. "Look at this!"

Burt peered at the handwriting. "What does it say? I can't read it."

"I wrote it myself. A bus ticket was discovered in the dead man's pocket. It was from Srinagar."

"Where's that?"

"In the disputed territory of Kashmir. Now I ask you, how do you know this man?" The officer was staring suspiciously at him now, waiting.

"I don't know him." Burt kept leafing through the rest of the pile, hoping to find a photo of Bobby. But there was none. "Do you remember a priest here about that time of this man's murder?"

"I think you have had your questions answered," the cop eyed him. "Now it is my turn. We think this man from Srinagar could have been a Separatist. Tell me, do you work with the Separatists?"

"I don't know anything about any Separatists." Burt said, "I'm an American. Just visiting."

"Then how do you know this man from Srinagar? Tell me the truth. Are you a Separatist? You know what happens to people who support them? I demand to see your passport and identification papers."

A muffled scream from outside made Burt swing around.

"Burt!" Lola pleaded.

He dashed through the front door. Outside, a gray-haired old woman in a black dress was dragging Lola away, kicking and fighting, her screams muffled now by a hand clamped on her mouth.

From behind, the Vespery policeman rushed out from the station, waving an ancient British military revolver. "You are being held for questioning, sir. Don't move!"

Lola momentarily tore free from the woman's grip and shouted, "She's *La Ombra*. I told you I saw her on the plane!"

Ignoring the cop, Burt rushed at the old woman. Seeing him coming, *La Ombra* lifted her long black skirt, ripped free the stiletto taped to her thigh and flung Lola aside.

Burt froze.

The Indian cop, seeing the knife, wheezed, "You there, put down that knife."

La Ombra lunged at Burt, slicing open the front of his Monaco t-shirt. He pulled back, startled at her speed.

The Indian cop, gun pointed, closed on the old woman. "I order you both in the name of the law to cease and desist. You are both under arrest!"

"Stay back!" Burt warned. "She's a killer!"

"And I, sir, am a trained police officer!"

To his surprise, he looked down to see a stiletto buried deep in his chest. His eyes grew big in shock as the assassin twisted her blade, then kicked him away as he fell.

Taking advantage of that moment, Burt lunged for the revolver the cop had dropped. He picked it up and pointed it at her. She hesitated, stiletto in hand, weighing her options.

"Come on," Burt told her. "Let me do it. I'll shoot you somewhere you live and tell me the truth."

"Before you pull the trigger, you'll be dead," she warned.

A crowd of curious shopkeepers, onlookers and their tuk-tuk driver was forming around them.

"Burt." Lola regained her feet. "Just kill her!"

"Not until I hear if she murdered Bobby." He cocked the gun. "You did it, didn't you!?"

"He was so afraid of me, he shat his pants." She laughed.

"So you killed him? He never committed suicide?"

In the distance, a siren began to wail.

"*Porca miseria*." Lola cried to Burt. "Now we should go." She swung up onto the seat of their rickshaw and started the tuk-tuk.

The driver objected, "You cannot take my taxi." But he kept his distance, standing up on the steps of the temple, too afraid to get closer to the stand-off that was taking place between the old woman with a knife and the man with a pistol.

The assassin smiled and lowered the knife to her side. "You want the truth? The truth is when I cornered him, I offered him myself. We went to a hotel. Afterwards, he was so ashamed, he killed himself. There, there's your truth."

She let the blade slide down her palm until her fingers held only the tip of the stiletto.

Lola cried, "Burt, watch out! It's an old trick! She's going to throw it."

La Ombra raised her hand to fling the blade. Burt pulled the trigger. The gun clicked, empty.

For a moment, the two enemies faced one another, astonished.

Lola cried out in dismay. "*Vacaggio!* That cop never loaded his gun!"

Burt tackled *La Ombra*, knocking the knife from her grip. He drove his fist into the killer's cheek. The stitch job she had done exploded in a mass of blood.

With the police sirens closing, Lola shouted, "Get in! If we don't go, we won't find what Bobby was after! Forget that *puta!*"

Hearing, Burt kicked her in the face, then jumped into the back of the tuk-tuk cab. As Lola drove away, he shouted at *La Ombra*, "This isn't finished, bitch!"

"Where do we go?" Lola asked over her shoulder as a green and white cop car swung into the plaza behind them.

Leaning forward, he shouted. "To a place called Srinagar. Wherever the hell that is."

CHAPTER TWENTY—FOUR

Indira Ghandi International Airport

Having lost Burt Powell and Lola Constantino in the usual terrible traffic, Inspector Jodpat and his assistant Nevo Muzzafaro received the horrible news that a fellow cop, Inspector Ruben Givas, had been discovered murdered on the arriving Lufthansa flight 113/1070 from Ankara, Turkey. Previously, Jodpat had been informed by headquarters in Lyons, France that Givas would be arriving in New Delhi today. But had not been told that he was aboard the same flight the two fugitives were on.

Standing now beneath the parked Lufthansa's 767's nose, Interpol Inspector Rohan Jodpat covered the body of Inspector Ruben Givas, his Spanish colleague, and ordered it loaded into the waiting morgue wagon.

"I cannot understand why he was aboard this flight," Jodpat said to his assistant. "Perhaps this is another coincidence?"

"This case seems full of them, sir," Muzzafaro offered. "Who else but these two fugitives could have killed him? They are very dangerous."

Jodpat turned and walked back toward the terminal, "A single, knowing thrust exactly between the ribs, into the heart? This man is a police officer. The other a student. No, this doesn't feel right, Nevo."

"Then who else could it be, sir?"

The Inspector's cell phone rang. "Jodpat," he answered. He listened, then disconnected.

"One of our own has been killed in Vespery."

"In the Old City?" Muzzafaro wondered. "Isn't that the precinct where that priest Father Bobby Powell committed suicide? And wasn't another man was murdered there too? Now one of our officers is killed in that same place. I believe this is all connected, sir!"

"We will have to find out," Jodpat and Muzzafaro climbed inside the police black Citroen and drove with its siren wailing. In about twenty minutes, they wound carefully through the tight alleys of the *Chandi Chowk* market place finally stopping in front of the Vespery police station.

Four constables in khaki had already cordoned the area off and were controlling the crime scene. Jodpat withdrew his Interpol badge and held it high. The constables recognized Inspector Jodpat and made way for him, opening a path through the throng of gawkers. Rohan approached the sprawled overweight corpse of the police officer lying in the street. He had been stripped naked, wearing now only his dirty underwear, shoes and socks.

Squatting beside him, Jodpat asked, "Who is this?"

"Officer Tamtam Aroha, sir." The Corporal, who was in charge, clicked his heels smartly, and answered.

"Where are his clothes?"

"No idea, sir. It is the way we found him."

"Any witnesses as to what happened?"

"Many, sir. But they ran away. Even the tuk-tuk driver who had his cab stolen, saw nothing."

Jodpat knew this was the way of India. Few witnesses came forward, unwilling to get involved in police matters.

He straightened and swept the scene with trained eyes, then bent, and withdrawing a pencil from his pocket, stuck it into the barrel of the dead officer's pistol. Peering at it, he saw that the revolver's chamber was empty. Just to be sure, he smelled the barrel.

"This hasn't been fired. And there are no cartridges in it."

"No, sir. He must have forgot to load it, sir," the Corporal said.

This did not surprise him. Most front desk cops were nothing more than bureaucrats. He doubted Officer Aroha had ever fired his weapon, much less felt like he needed he had to. The rust spots along the pistol confirmed he had also never bothered to maintain it properly.

The Corporal checked his notes. "As I mentioned, there is a driver, sir. He says a young woman stole his *tuk-tuk*."

"Where is he?"

"Gone, now. I ordered him to stay. But he slipped away. We will find him, sir."

"Did you interview him and get a description of the thief?"

"Yes, most certainly. And he described the woman as young."

"Young, you've already said that."

"Uh. there was a man here too. He fought an old woman who had a knife. And drove off with the young woman in the taxi cab."

"The man and old woman were fighting?"

"Yes, sir. He had the officer's gun and she had a knife."

"The gun was empty."

"Yes, sir. I was unable to find out what happened. Only that they had those weapons."

Jodpat looked exasperated. "Anything else to report, Corporal?"

"Yes, sir. The old woman wore a black dress and dropped the knife. A long thin dagger, sir. We found it. "

For the first time, Jodpat showed genuine interest as the constable handed him the stiletto. He peered at the dagger inside the glassine evidence bag. "A carefully designed weapon," he said.

"Perhaps, sir," Muzzafaro, his assistant who had stood silently by now suggested. "The kind that could have been used to kill Interpol Inspector Givas aboard the plane?"

"You are reaching, Nevo. But we shall see. Put out an All-Points Bulletin for the old woman, as well as the thieves who stole the tuk-tuk. Tell them to look for someone wearing Officer Aroha's uniform."

The Corporal said, "With all due respect, sir, while we have been ordered to cooperate with Interpol, it has no authority here."

"You are correct," Jodpat admitted. "Will you tell your superior I *suggest* you look for someone in Aroha's uniform?"

"I will do that," the constable saluted smartly and left.

Muzzafaro asked, "The two we were waiting for and who gave us the slip at the airport were the ones here, sir? I mean we know that the priest who died was Burt Powell's brother. There is no doubt this was their destination."

"Burt Powell and Lola Constantino," Rohan said their names out loud meditatively. He walked a few feet away, studying the scene, "And the old woman? How does she figure in this?"

Muzzafaro shrugged. "She is, as they say, a new player, sir."

"Go through the passenger list aboard the flight Givas was murdered. We need to know if there was an old woman on that Lufthansa plane. I want a copy of her passport photo."

"There will be more than one old woman, sir. There might even be fifty or a hundred. This could take some time."

"I know that, Nevo. After you gather them all, get Interpol in Lyons to identify each one."

"Sir." Muzzafaro obeyed and ran back to the police car to radio in his boss's instructions.

Jodpat pulled open the door to the Vespery police station. Entering, he walked behind the scarred front counter and spotted a pile of paper. One page was pulled out. He picked it up. It was the photo of the unidentified Indian in the white robe, murdered here.

Turning it over, he saw that Officer Aroha had made a notation. In his wobbly, kindergarten handwriting, he had scrawled, "Effects on body, one bus ticket, from and to Srinagar."

The Inspector frowned. If the American cop was here investigating why his brother died, it stood to reason that if he read this report and learned that the man was from Kashmir, he would go there, would he not? Or would he?

Perhaps this was nothing more than a red herring. Perhaps it was Aroha, the desk cop merely reviewing his cases. Or perhaps the American cop's brother had nothing to do with this murdered man from Kashmir.

But what other lead was there? If he failed to act, the case could be at a dead end. Well, he had been wrong before. But one thing was certain. Inspector Rohan Jodpat could not be accused of being afraid to have a little egg on his face.

Folding the photo, Jodpat strode back out into the bazaar.

"Muzzafaro!" he shouted. "We must go to Kashmir."

Hearing that, his assistant, finishing the call into the office, blanched. Looking ashen, he asked, "Kashmir? Why there, sir?"

"Because I have a hunch. And hunches and coincidences are what we trade in. Now fill out a requisition report and see if our meager Interpol budget will allow us to take the chopper."

CHAPTER TWENTY—FIVE

With Burt seated in the *tuk-tuk* canopy behind her, Lola drove along the banks of the fetid and polluted Yamuna River. Truckloads of trash and rotting garbage lined its banks and floated in the brown, sluggish water. Children were swimming in the river, diving for coins beneath a wrought-iron bridge, dropped there for good luck by passersby above. Beggars, with horrible deformities of leprosy, leaned against the bridge's pilings, stubs of arms extended hoping to catch stray rupees.

Momentarily, as they passed under the bridge, Burt wondered if this was where they had found Bobby hanging. He leaned forward and said to Lola, "We should ditch this taxi."

With the traffic growing heavier as they headed back into New Delhi, Lola, spotting a bunch of trees in a vacant field, pulled off the road and hid the rickshaw there.

"Where's this Srinagar?" she swung off the driver's seat and walked away with Burt.

"The cop said it was in Kashmir."

"Isn't that where Haijar reported Mary's tribe lived?"

"Right," Burt shook his head.

After they had walked several blocks in silence, Burt said, "I can't get over letting her get away. I had her!"

"You hurt her pretty bad."

"If I had had more time..." he stopped himself. "Lola, look, maybe you've done enough. I'll take it from here."

"You think I'm going to quit now?" she said.

He nodded and reaching out, squeezed her hand. In an industrial section where workers were smelting bars of aluminum, they stopped at a street vendor's cart and bought bottles of warm water. Burt asked him directions to Srinagar.

"You don't want to go there. Very dangerous, very, very bad place." he shook his head. "Big war, everyone killing each other. Pakistanis against Indians. Terrible place."

"We have to go there," Lola told him.

The Indian clucked his tongue. "Well, if it is your destiny. Then you have no choice. You must go."

"What's the best way to get there?" Burt wondered.

"Plane."

"No good," Burt shook his head. And Lola understood that an airport would be the first place the police would look for them.

"What else?"

The Indian thought a moment then his eyes lit up. "Bus!" He pointed to an enormous billboard across the street. The sign blared, "Go with The Best. India National Tours."

"It is just up the street. Very famous. The best Religious tours ever! I take it every year for my pilgrimage." He pointed and they turned to look at a gaudy yellow, purple and red building at the end of a dirt road, its lot filled with buses.

CHAPTER TWENTY—SIX

Inside the India Tours bus terminal, women in yellow saris, men in long white robes pressed toward ticket counters. The room was painted in garish red and purple, with loud Bollywood music blaring from the speakers. Burt and Lola pushed forward and finally when it was their turn, arrived at one of the ticket vendors.

"We'd like to get to Srinagar." Lola told the cashier.

"Ah. Kashmir. Do you know where that is?"

"You tell us," Burt said.

"It is 400 kilometers north. But I cannot issue you a ticket for there. Go over there to that man, Mr. Nair at his desk in the corner. He is an expert who handles that area."

At his desk, Mr. Nair, in his business suit, greeted them effusively, promising that the trip from New Delhi to Srinagar was a wonderful experience and that it would only take twenty-four hours. "Very safe. Lots of soldiers guarding the roads. No problem."

"Soldiers?" Burt frowned.

"It is beautiful this time of year in Kashmir." the ticket seller assured them. "Have you seen the houseboats on Dal lake? Did you ever stroll beneath the *Takhat Sulaiman,* the Throne of Solomon? A most magnificent temple. Built in 54 A.D. Don't worry, it is most safe and enjoyable."

"Kashmir's a war zone." Burt told him. "We will worry."

"Ah, the food is wonderful." he ignored Burt's comment and smiled smarmily. "You will have a most delightful time. MasterCard, Visa, American Express or cash?"

Handing the agent his MasterCard, tickets were quickly issued. "Now, follow me, please, this way."

Burt and Lola traded looks as the agent took them out the back door into a gigantic parking lot where hundreds of India National Tour buses were parked and being loaded with people who were all dressed in exactly the same flowing white robes.

"Your bus number is number seventy-three." The agent pointed down a long line through the crowd thronging the lot.

"Who are all these people?" Lola wondered seeing the white-robed passengers clambering onto buses.

"Ah, those are the Hindu Amaranth pilgrims," the tour guide smiled proudly "They have rented one hundred and forty-seven buses. But your number seventy-three will of course stop in Srinagar then travel on another forty-five kilometers into the high mountains. Now, board and enjoy air conditioning bliss. Very comfortable."

Inside their assigned bus, there was no difference between the sweltering heat and humidity outside. In fact, it was, with the press and smell of bodies, even hotter and more miserable. Some of its occupants were actually dancing and singing in the aisles, like they were on holiday.

Finding two empty seats at the rear, Lola asked a woman with a red dot on her forehead, "What's going on?"

"We are Hindi," she giggled happily, "going on our annual pilgrimage. We call it *yatra.*"

"*Yatra?* What's that?"

"We go to the sacred shrine."

"What shrine?"

The man sitting next to her happily explained. "The holy shrine of Shiva, big god of the Hindu Trinity. We do pilgrimage to Shiva to pay our tribute of *darshan.*" He stuck out his hand. "I am Subas, this is Davia." He grinned proudly. "It is our eighth year attending."

Davia added shyly, "The ice lingam this year is fourteen feet tall. Very propitious for fertility." She looked at her husband coyly.

"Last year there was nothing." her husband said. "This year, we are very fortunate and blessed. It is a prosperous sign indeed from Lord Shiva."

"What's a lingam?" Lola whispered to Burt. "I don't know that word."

To which, Davia overhearing, said, "It's a phallus."

"Phallus?" Lola looked more confused.

Davia dug in her bag and produced a photo of a huge, ice stalagmite rising from the floor of a cave. "Here. It is Lord Shiva's holy cock."

"*Che cazzo.*" Lola's eyes widened. "It is the size of a missile."

The wife laughed lustfully and again looked at her husband, eyes twinkling. "*Bom Bom Bhole.*" she said.

"*Bom Bom Bhole.*" he replied and kissed her.

"What do those words mean?" Lola asked.

Davia giggled, "*Bom Bom* is the cosmic rhythm of sex that Shiva makes when he plays his drum. It is his dance of unending creation."

"And *Bhole,*" her husband Subas added. "It means do it again. And again."

They both burst into laughter.

In a few minutes, the bus lumbered out of the lot. As they entered the main highway that fed out of New Delhi, a police car screamed past the bus, sirens wailing. Burt looked at Lola, both of them holding their breath, expecting to be stopped and searched. But the car sped on.

They rode silently into open country, both tired and emotionally exhausted.

The crowded buses that had departed the India Tours in New Delhi stayed together in a long line as they rumbled up a long winding road that fed high into the mountains. Snowy peaks over twenty thousand feet hung above them as the buses climbed.

Inside bus seventy-three, the pilgrims had settled down and people were eating and were quietly engaged in conversation.

Lola asked Burt, "What were you doing before you were a cop?"

Momentarily, Burt looked startled. Then he said, "Why do you ask?"

"A cop isn't trained to do the things you have done. Like count your footsteps in the cave. Push past the pain and shock of being shot."

He kept his face turned away, then finally seemed to make up his mind. "You want my trust."

"Yes."

"I've never told anyone this. Not even my wife, Francie."

"Why?"

"Because she would have despised me."

He looked away again, kept his face toward the window. "I was in a unit that didn't officially exist. We were called Tiger One because of what we were trained to do. Our job was to parachute into enemy territory, before the main invasion. Spread mayhem."

"Mayhem? What does that mean?"

"It means I hid alone during the day, moved through the night. Left the enemy hanging by their own guts. Gouged out eyes, cut out tongues, put brains, fingers, toes in their food and boots, hacked off genitalia and shoved it in dead men's mouths. My job was to spread terror and confusion. To make them jumpy, trigger happy, soften them up."

"I never knew of such a job."

"Most people lead ordinary lives and have no idea of what evil is out there. I was trained to match that. I got no respect from my fellow soldiers who knew what I did. Other guys stayed away from us, called us creepy, said we were like hyenas. We didn't even exist on paper. I was deniable. At the end of the war, out of the twenty-six who started, there were only two of us left."

"Che un incubo terribile."

He turned finally and looked at her, waiting for the translation.

"A terrible nightmare," she translated.

He nodded. "A nightmare. We called ourselves the Ghoul Squad."

"You told the truth when you said you and Bobby were not alike."

"Twins. But different as night and day." He paused. "Now you have my trust too."

"And together we will bring Bobby justice." Lola leaned over and kissed him on the mouth. *"Bom Bom,"* she said.

At first he looked surprised, but after a beat, grinned and replied, *"Bhole!"*

***

They turned off the highway onto a rough gravel road, filled with potholes. Repeatedly, the bus was obliged to stop at military checkpoints and each time all passengers were required to get off and show their passports. This happened at the borders of India, Pakistan, and finally, about midnight, at the Kashmir crossing station.

The road grew even rougher and narrower as they climbed higher, then abruptly descended into a deep valley with thousand foot drop-offs alongside the bus. In the moonlight, Subas pointed out the great Karakoram range snowy peaks running above them, indicating in the distance the frosted mountains of Everest, K-2 and Nanga Parbat.

Now, more stern-faced Indian soldiers began to show up along the high mountain road, patrolling, armed with Kalashnikovs. It seemed they were everywhere on the roads. Entire army convoys were clustered together, filled with wary military.

Subas, seeing their concerned looks, said, "Thirty- seven pilgrims were killed by Kashmiri Separatists last year. But don't worry, we are being protected. The Lord Shiva has asked us to take this journey. He will keep us safe."

"Where exactly is his ice cave?" Lola asked.

Davia said, "Past Srinagar, then onward to his holy mountain called Baltal. There we hike to 11,000 feet and, if we are invited, enter Shiva's cave."

"You mean you could go all that way and not get inside?" Burt was amazed.

"A priest there will determine if we are worthy. If not, we cannot enter."

"Like Saint Peter at the pearly gates," Burt told the couple who looked confused.

"It's a joke," Lola explained. "St. Peter stands in front of heaven and admits only those who have been good."

"Ah, I understand! Saint Peter. He is like Shiva." Davia cried out, understanding. *"Har Mahadev."*

The entire bus roared back, *"Jai Baba Barfani. Bom Bhole."* And everyone broke into song.

CHAPTER TWENTY—SEVEN

Vatican City, Rome

That evening, leaving the Palace of the Holy Office, seat of the Congregation for the Doctrine of Faith, once called the fearsome Holy Office of the Inquisition, its current head, Cardinal Giuseppe Montalvo, strode across the tourist-filled *Piazza San Pietro*, the main square that faced the city and fed into the basilica. Because his offices were actually located outside the Vatican wall, Montalvo was forced to enter the actual papal grounds through a gate.

He might have gone through the closest one which was the *Via Della Campane,* but chose instead to stretch his legs across the huge *piazza* and walk north to St. Anne's gate. As usual, that entrance was manned by a squad of Swiss Guards, dressed in their smart new blue uniforms. Long ago, they had given up the yellow and black medieval regalia, complete with silver breastplate and helmet, associated with that elite force who guarded the Vatican.

Receiving their salutes, Cardinal Montalvo strode into the Vatican city past the Guards' barracks on Belvedere, then swung right at the printing offices of the Vatican newspaper, cut through the auto park, which at this hour was nearly empty because most civilian employees had finished their day and gone home and at last, turning into *Salita dei Giardini,* his favorite gardens, filled with cottonwoods that sang a sweet song in the breeze, he climbed a set of narrow steps into the Borgia Courtyard, then ascended finally into the *Cortile Libreria,* the vast Vatican libraries.

At the entrance, another Swiss Guard on duty saluted him, then pulled open its heavy black steel door admitting the prelate into a dimly lit foyer. There, Montalvo was immediately greeted by Monsignor Anselmo Tuppo who had been waiting.

"*Signore.*" He bowed and kissed his ruby ring.

They walked a few steps together and entered a low door, designed for when people were shorter, then came into the ancient vast Vatican library itself.

Towering above and all around them, oaken wood shelves rose three stories from floor to ceiling, with over 1.1 million sacred and profane printed books. Included also were the 8500 *incunabula,* which were single sheets and drawings copied before 1501 A.D. and 75,000 rare manuscripts, dating back thousands of years, each illuminated and copied by monks.

Cardinal Montalvo ran his eyes over the happy treasures. How he loved this place of history, so solemn, so grand, filled with such wisdom. Every great work of mankind, every religious piece of writing, every blessed and condemned tract, from the forbidden Egyptian *Book of the Dead* to Galileo's theory that the sun did not revolve around the earth, had been collected here in this one spot.

The Cardinal settled himself on a bare, marble bench beneath the looming shelves, took a deep breath and said, "I have just learned that *La Ombra* has been injured and requests our assistance. She needs medical help. And money."

"Where is she at this moment, *Eminencia?*" Monsignor Tuppo asked. Even though he was a member of the *Manus Christi,* the Hand of Christ, and had requested this campaign against these heretics who had stolen the *Yuz Asaf,* he was genuinely flattered to be included by the Cardinal in this ongoing process. Normally, once a case was opened, Cardinal Montalvo, the head of the Hand of Christ secretly handled everything.

"*La Ombra* is presently in New Delhi, at the hospital of Our Little Sisters of Mercy. Her nose is broken and she has a large, infected wound on her face, received, I was told, from an animal attack at Tarsus."

"The animals broke her nose also?"

"She only mentioned the wound on her face."

"Did she retrieve the document?"

"She says she was close. But the American brother of the heretic thief got away."

"To where may I ask?"

"She does not know. And now she must find out. That is why I came to you. What does the wretched *Yuz Asaf* document say? Any clues? You are the expert, Monsignor."

"It says that Jesus went to that contested area between India, China and Pakistan, called today, Kashmir. Though of course I do not believe Jesus went there."

"Of course not. A question that has occurred to me, Anselmo. I have often wondered how that this young priest..." He searched for a name.

"Father Robert Powell."

"Yes, I have wondered, how he gained admittance into the secret section of our archives?"

"You remember that after Pope John Paul II threw the doors open, Eminence, I was besieged with requests from scholars to look at ancient heretical texts. Of course I resisted, offering reasons why no one should be permitted to gain access. But this Father Powell, who after all, had an unsavory reputation of researching areas of our faith such as the Shroud of Turin and the *Sudarium,* the Holy Veil of St Veronica, that should have been left alone, turned for help to American Cardinal Mahan. In short, I was forced to give in and allow him inside."

"It is a rule we must change after we clean up this mess. That section must once again be closed. Tell me, Anselmo, are you familiar with all of the *Yuz Asaf's* particulars?"

"I studied it briefly before I first filed it away."

"Aside from the writing in the document," Montalvo rose and ambled slowly across the parquet floor of the vast library. "if Jesus, or somebody they thought was Jesus, came long ago to Kashmir, there would be evidence of it. Perhaps even a tomb?" Montalvo stopped dead. "With bones."

"Eminence, please, there was no mention of a tomb or bones. This is all nonsense."

"You're sure? But what if there are bones, Anselmo?"

"Even so, who would believe such a fairy tale that the bones belonged to Jesus? What proof could there be? Who would believe it?"

The Cardinal replied, "Of course, no one would *believe* it. The question is, would it cause a significant doubt? Faith is a fragile thing, Anselmo. Remember, in trial, a clever defense attorney, to win his case, must only place a single doubt in a jury's mind. And in this case, unless firmly dis-proven, a small doubt could grow like the proverbial mustard seed into disastrous consequences."

He paused, staring down the long darkened hallway that connected this "A" wing with seven others. "Do not underestimate the power of uncertainty, Anselmo. No matter how preposterous a concept, once skepticism sets in, and the rational mind takes over, doubt can spread like a cancer."

Tuppo saw the veins on the Cardinal's forehead engorge as he spoke passionately. "Always, doubt, remains our constant enemy, Monsignor. If you doubt, you begin to ask questions. Why would a loving Father make his Son die for him? To forgive the sins of the world? What an ego. What kind of monster is such a Father?"

"Blasphemous thoughts, Eminence." Tuppo caught his breath.

"And yet, Anselmo, and yet, there are so many things a rational mind can pick out in scripture and holy doctrine. Things that make a mind wonder. Like, why are there only four gospels, when once there was a total of fifty-six? Fifty-two condemned by the early church, declared heretical and ordered destroyed. Yet they were written by holy men and women such as Mary Magdalen, Phillip, Thomas, who knew Christ? Why was this done? I will tell you. Because they either directly contradicted what Paul and the four gospel writers set down or forgot to mention that Jesus was Christ and that he died on the cross to save the world from its sins. "

"There are always instances where the gospels disagree or contradict one another. It doesn't invalidate them."

"The point I am making is, because believers want to cheat death and rise up with their immortal souls and go to an eternal life, they are willing to overlook inconsistencies. But if it ever came out that Jesus never died at all, never saved them on the cross, never rose again, and the Church lied about it all, well, even the most faithful would turn away from us and rise up in a justified rage."

Taking a deep, shuddering breath, the cardinal, withdrew a scarlet lace handkerchief from his red cassock pocket, blew his large aquiline nose, and said, "Send *La Ombra* money. Give her anything she needs. We must dispose of this grave matter quickly. Thank you for your information, Anselmo."

Lifting his scarlet robes, the Prince of the Church swept to the doorway of the Vatican Library and Archives. There, he paused and turned. "Our annual world membership of *Manus Christi* meets in one week in Malta. There will be many powerful donors there. I want to use that occasion to announce the end of this affair. Do I make myself clear, Monsignor?"

"Very, Eminence." Tuppo bowed.

CHAPTER TWENTY—EIGHT

New Delhi, India

The helicopter landed on the roof of the Little Sisters of Mercy hospital and *La Ombra* ran to board it. Having abandoned the fat policeman's khaki uniform she had taken in Vespery, the assassin now sported the white outfit of a nurse with a scarlet cape fastened at her neck by a gold chain. On the front of the cape, she had ordered a Red Crescent patch, which she had spotted on a blanket in the hospital. This symbol was the Islamic mirror organization of the Red Cross. Not only was it the cover *La Ombra* needed, but the Red Crescent, like the Christian countries' sacred use of the insignia of the Red Cross, would be respected. She had also taken the added precaution of dyeing her blond hair black, actually its original color.

Of course, none of the kind nuns who had helped her and were now waving goodbye as the chopper lifted off the roof knew anything about who she was or her mission. After leaving the Vespery police station, her nose bleeding and broken, *La Ombra* had huddled beneath the pilings of a bridge she had strung the heretic priest on and called Cardinal Giuseppe Montalvo in Rome. In short order, the nuns at the Little Sisters of Mercy Hospital had received an important phone call from Vatican City and were informed they must send a car to rescue an injured member of the Vatican. They were also told that Delicata Fabrizio should be given anything she required.

Once at the hospital, after a surgeon set her broken nose and irrigated and re-stitched the wound on her cheek, *La Ombra* had texted her data nerds in Lausanne, requesting they do a background search on the Indian she had murdered in front of the temple. In less than an hour, data appeared, complete with photo snatched from the electronic files of the New Delhi Police. The Indian was identified as Kali Mohi and was from Srinagar in Kashmir. So now she knew where her pigeons were going.

Overruling the doctor's orders to stay in the hospital, face puffy and covered with a skin tone bandage, which she had insisted over a white one, broken nose set, newly disguised as an Islamic nurse, *La Ombra* seated herself beside the pilot the Hand of Christ had hired. He informed her it would be one hour flying time to Srinagar.

As the chopper shook and shimmied its way up into the high mountains, the vibrations of the blades coursed through her bones, causing her cheek and nose to throb. As usual, to keep her mind clear, she had refused any pain medication. But despite all the pain she was suffering, a mellow sense of satisfaction began to smooth her jagged senses. She was close, very close.

Flying up through high mountain passes, *La Ombra* again text messaged her International Database unit in Switzerland, requesting them to supply her with intelligence on the current military situation in Kashmir. She then received and read several articles they relayed back to her, quickly acquainting herself with the ongoing war. Kashmir had for years been contested by India and Pakistan. Muslims were trapped on the Indian side and Hindus on the Pakistani. To complicate matters, there was an internal civil war, led by Separatists. In short, Kashmir was a complicated mess. She would have to be very careful.

Reading further, the Shadow learned that while the number of ambushes from Separatists had declined in Kashmir, there were still many incidents of Indian soldiers being attacked and murdered. The BSF, the official Border Security Force of India, with its 200,000 paramilitary combatants assigned to protect its border, had responded by shooting on sight Pashtun jihadists, Kashmir Separatists, killing also in the process many innocent men, women and children. The result was a trigger-happy tension with the Kashmir people who wanted independence from India and hated its occupiers. Despite the danger, it was perfect, *La Ombra* decided. Anyone could die here and their deaths would go unnoticed.

***

Beneath the majestic peaks of the Himalayas, in the cool, late afternoon sunlight, on one of Srinagar's nine bridges that spanned the glacier-fed *Jhelum* river, Burt and Lola de-boarded from the bus, waved goodbye to Davia and Subas and picked their way through the cobblestone rubble that had been blown up by mortar shells.

It was ironic how beautiful the valley of Srinagar was, a veritable paradise, and yet it was a battlefield. Every building they passed was burnt out, or surrounded by sandbags and razor wire. Deserted streets were lined with jumpy Indian soldiers who patrolled and guarded them. There was an electric tension in the air, as if at any moment, something bad was going to happen.

"This doesn't get any easier," Lola noted.

On the hillsides above, large, Western style vacation houses, stood wrecked, windows broken, empty and in disrepair. Subas and Davia had pointed out these houses, explaining many were abandoned, filled now with squatters and homeless victims of the ongoing conflict between India and Pakistan over this land called Kashmir.

On the bus, Subas, at hearing from Burt that they were stopping in Srinagar, had kindly written down various tourist sites for them to enjoy: the Dal lake, the floating gardens, the rich food, the exotic music.

Lola said, "We've come to see if Jesus was here. Not eat or dance."

"Then there is a pillar you must see, in the Temple of Solomon, inscribed in 54 A.D. Here, look." He dug in their backpack and retrieved a Kashmir travel guide, then locating the right page, tapped his finger on a black and white photo. "This writing is inscribed on one of the temple columns. It states Jesus was there in 54 A.D."

Burt and Lola stared at the old picture of a pillar with the words chiseled on its base: '*Dar een waqt Yuz Asaf da'wa-i-paighambari mikunad, Sal punjah wa chakar.*' which means, Subas translated, 'At this time, *Yuz Asaf* proclaimed his prophethood, in the year fifty and four.'"

He continued, "'*Aishan Yusu Paighambar-i-Bani Israel ast.*' That says "He is Jesus, Prophet of the Children of Israel.'"

"His tomb is in town," Davia revealed. "Though we have never seen it."

Lola and Burt exchanged a long look.

Now, picking their way through the rubble and burned out hulks of tanks and cars left on the streets, Burt and Lola approached an Indian officer on a bridge.

Gruffly, he demanded, "Passports."

After viewing them, and satisfied that Burt and Lola did not appear to be Separatist guerrillas, the officer said, "Why are you here?"

"We're pilgrims," Lola said. "Come to see the tomb of Jesus."

"Issa's tomb? Why?"

"To offer our prayers," Burt answered quickly.

"You realize this city is under curfew? Do you see anyone on the street? No one is allowed on the streets."

"We'll make it quick."

The officer looked them over one more time. "You have only a few hours before sunset. Do not be on the street at nightfall or you will be shot. The tomb is in the *Khanyar* district, 150 meters past the *Dastgir Saheb* mosque. Up that hill." He waved his hand toward an ascent in the road, then handing back their passports, strode away.

They climbed the cracked road, picking their way between garbage that littered the street. At the top of the hill, in a strange twist of war, they spotted kids playing soccer with a beat-up ball.

Lola approached one and asked, "*Yuz Asaf?*"

One of the boys brightened and pointed up the road, saying, "*Youza Asouph.*" He ran ahead as if to show them the way.

Burt and Lola followed him, stepping over more trash, twisted pieces of water pipe and scraps of lumber. Some of the little shacks lining the street had been blown up by bombs and heavy artillery.

Turning a corner, they saw the boy had stopped in front of a small house that had been once been painted green and pink. Now its walls were chipped from small arms fire, its paint was peeling and like many other battered buildings, it was surrounded by barb wire.

As they approached the high, outside wall, the boy pointed to a battered, hand painted sign stating, "*Youza Asouph Hazrat Issa Sahib.*"

"This can't be the tomb." Burt said. "It's a shack."

You are wrong. It is *Hazrat Issa Sahib,* Tomb of the

Lord Master Jesus." an English voice behind them said. They spun and saw a lovely woman sticking her head out of a badly damaged house across the street.

"This is the tomb of Jesus?" Lola asked doubtfully.

"Along with the Muslim Saint, *Syed Nasir-Ud-Din,* a descendant of Mohammad. They lie side by side."

"Can we get inside?" Burt asked.

"It is locked." She strode into the street and the boy ran and stood beside her.

"Who has the key?"

"My husband was keeper of the key. Now I suppose I am." Her face looked strained. "You had better come inside. "It is nearly dark and curfew will begin. You should come inside before the fighting begins again."

***

When the rented chopper landed at the Government Medical College and the pilot had shut down the engines, members of the Indian Border Security Forces appeared and surrounded it. *La Ombra* had anticipated this and alighting, told the officer, that as a Muslim nurse she had come to see what medical supplies were needed for civilian casualties. This seemed to please the officer and he led her across an expanse of cement to a nearby children's school which had been transformed into BSF headquarters. Its front was pockmarked with bullets. A sign, blown off its supports, leaned against its entrance, stating "United India Border Security Force."

Pushing inside its gloomy front entrance which was piled with sandbags blocking light from the windows, *La Ombra* followed the officer as he spoke to a clerk behind a desk. The Indian official adjusted his red cravat inside his khaki uniform, rose and knocking on a double door behind him, went inside.

In a moment, a Colonel with gold braids on his shoulders and a myriad of campaign medals, emerged. "May I help you?" he asked *La Ombra*. Without responding, she walked past him into his office.

The Colonel frowned and went back inside. He found the woman, already seated before his desk which was awkwardly positioned in the middle of an oversized room that had once served as the grade school's cafeteria. Only the warped linoleum floor and banged up stainless steel serving counters remained.

The officer seated himself behind his desk. "This is most irregular."

La Ombra said, "Once you hear what I have to say, you will realize why I insist on privacy." She paused, as if searching for the right words, "First off, I am not a nurse."

"Then who are you? And why are you here wearing this trickery?" The officer's voice had an edge.

In answer, *La Ombra* reached into her pocket and withdrew one million rupees, about twenty-five thousand dollars and laid it on the Colonel's desk.

"What is this?" he asked.

"For you."

"I could have you arrested. Bribing a senior officer is punishable by death. You could be shot by a firing squad."

"You wouldn't do such a stupid thing without hearing me out."

The officer, actually not a full Colonel, but a Lieutenant Colonel, asked, "Again who are you?"

"You do not need to know that."

"I will know what I need. And believe me I can get it out of you," he said. "And you are not in charge here." He peered at her bandaged cheek. "What happened to your face?"

"An accident."

"I am familiar with wounds. That is a deep one."

"My clients are powerful and immensely wealthy. They would be very angry if you dismissed my request out of hand without hearing it."

The Lieutenant Colonel leaned forward. "I am a soldier, veteran of many battlefields. And I tell you now, whoever your clients are, they do not scare me."

La Ombra's voice echoed across the empty room. "The moment I entered this school and saw your desk in the middle of this cafeteria, I knew it was not a proper office for someone of your high rank. It is clearly an act of disrespect."

She saw his eyes move to the stack of money. "What do you want?"

"I need someone to show me where the so-called tomb of Jesus is, if there is such a thing."

"It exists." He stared at the stack of bills. "Is that all?"

La Ombra hid her surprise. She had found the truth so easily. Could this really be what the Hand of Christ feared the world might find?

"Colonel Bagh," La Ombra read the name tag on his chest. "Do you believe Jesus could really be inside this tomb?"

The Colonel whose full name was Nasim Bagh shrugged. "I can't say. However, it is also believed that the tomb of his mother, Mary lies in the nearby town of Muree. And another tomb in *Taxbar* holds Mary Magdalen's remains. Again, this is all conjecture. And being Muslim, I have never explored it."

"One more thing, in what I am here to do, you must tell your men to leave me alone."

Lieutenant Colonel Bagh said, "I could lose my rank for such a thing."

La Ombra shrugged and reached for the money.

The Colonel said quickly, "I am fifty-six, near retirement. And do you know what awaits me? A little house and an ugly wife with a meager pension that will not buy toilet paper sufficient to wipe my ass."

"Then you deserve this," *La Ombra* cooed sympathetically, pushing the bundle of cash toward him.

The Colonel frowned but slid the rupees into his top drawer. Closing it, he said, "Whoever you are, you have one hour. After that, I do not know you."

La Ombra rose. "One more thing. Have you been notified of the arrival of two travelers, an American man and young Italian woman?"

The Colonel swiveled to his desk top Acer, and hit a button. "Captain Priit on the Jhelum bridge reported they were seen less than an hour ago."

CHAPTER TWENTY—NINE

Once inside the simple concrete block house, they saw there was no furniture, just a few worn large pillows tossed onto a cracked cement floor. The boy followed them and sat down on one.

"He is my son, Father." the woman said, "I am Chakri."

Lola introduced themselves. Burt spotted a familiar photo of an Indian man that was placed in a little alcove in the wall, surrounded by lit candles. Freshly strewn orange chrysanthemums lay before it. "I know this man," he said.

Chakri gasped. "He is my husband, Kali. Do you know something about him? He has been missing for nearly a month now. And we have received no word." The woman, afraid of what she was about to hear, cringed. She saw Burt and Lola hesitate, and glance at her son. "Pather does not speak English," she said. "Tell me."

"We think your husband died possibly with my brother, Father Bobby Powell, in Delhi." Burt found his voice.

Chakri stiffened. "Please," she said after a moment,

"for the sake of my son, show no emotion. I will smile as I hear what you have to say. I will tell him later. Already, he does not sleep and is very worried about his father."

"What did your husband do here in Sringar?" Lola asked.

Chakri kissed her son and continued, "In addition to being the gatekeeper here at the tomb, Kali had a part-time job at the University in Srinagar. It was my husband's duty to assist Dr. Izmet Hisban, head of the Archeology Department in his research on cataloging various site digs in Kashmir. Dr. Hisban's intention was to perform an archaeological dig on Issa's tomb to verify its authenticity."

"And did he?" Lola was interested.

"No," Chakri said. "The local Muslim Imams forbade honoring the tomb. You must realize it is forbidden for Muslims to believe that Jesus never rose from the dead."

"Why?" Lola looked surprised.

"Because they thought he was a great prophet and his body, like Muhammed's, was in heaven." Chakri smiled reassuringly at Pather who was trying to figure out what was being said, but could not.

"I know," she continued, "that Father Bobby sent requests by e-mail to several Universities in India asking for information concerning the tomb of Issa. When Kali saw one arrive in the local University's email box here, he immediately contacted him."

"That's what Hana told us." Lola said. "It was Kali who contacted Bobby and told him where Jesus had journeyed to."

"And I know," Chakri confirmed, "that he journeyed to New Delhi to meet him,"

Burt asked, "But why did Kali meet him in New Delhi? Bobby should just have come directly here to the Tomb."

Chakri said, "Someone had called Dr. Hisban's office, saying the Separatists had plans to blow up the tomb,"

"So how was he going to save the tomb by meeting Bobby in New Delhi? That doesn't make sense."

"I don't know." Chakri paused. "Tell me, where is my husband's body? I must go and bring him home."

"We know only that he was killed in the Chandi Chowk market place. Currently, he is unidentified."

"I will go there tomorrow and ask for him. I'm sure the police will tell me what morgue he lies in."

"Is it possible to visit the tomb?" Lola asked. "We have come such a long way and the journey has been very perilous."

"There is just enough daylight left, I think. But as I said you must be off the streets before night comes." Chakri ducked into a back room.

Lola crossed to look at an embroidered cloth hanging on a wall that said, "*Bnei Menash.*"

"Bnet Menash," Pather announced proudly.

"Mary's tribe." Lola put it together.

When Chakri reappeared, Lola asked her, "Are you part of the *Bnei Menash* tribe?"

"Yes, and my husband is, or was, a direct descendant of Jesus, peace be upon him."

Burt stared at Pather. "Then so is your son."

Chakri smiled, "He is of a long lineage." She held out an old brass key. "Now, hurry. Go quickly. And let no one see you enter."

CHAPTER THIRTY

As Burt and Lola left the little house and hurried across the street to the sorry little structure, they saw that behind the high, rusting iron fence with spikes was a sign stating *Hazrat Issa Sahib, No Visitors Allowed.*

"Nothing like a friendly welcome," Burt said. Checking around, he inserted the key into a centuries-old lock on the gate and pushed it open.

"The sun's setting," Lola checked the horizon. "We only have a few minutes."

"We'll make it fast."

They quickly moved to the front door of the little building. It too was locked. Burt tried the key but it didn't fit. He brought up his foot and kicked the wobbly door open. It fell off its hinges and crashed down.

"Desecration," Lola muttered.

"Call it what you want. We're in."

Entering a small courtyard, they saw that there were two coffins lying inside a rectangular enclosure behind a scratched up wall of Plexiglass.

Lola approached the first clouded pane and peered inside. She could make out a green stone sarcophagus. Next to it was a smaller one. She looked up on the wall. A faded sign read. *"Tarikh-I-Kashmir,* "A*t the age of thirty-three years, Issa proceeded from Palestine to this Holy Valley."*

"Issa, Haijar, was the name for Jesus," she recalled.

Cupping her hands, Lola peered through the dirty glass. "Look, I can see two carved feet on the top, each bearing a nail wound. It means this man was crucified."

Burt moved to the next Plexiglass window with a new sign. *"From the Khuda Baksh Library in Patna, India,"* he read, *"the Book of Balauhar, 47 A.D. 'At last Issa reached the capital city. He called all people to the Kingdom of God and stayed there until the last day of his life. He preached that it is necessary to follow the Commandments of God.*

And that none should go toward untruth, leaving the Truth. To adhere to prayer and hold fast to the Truth'."

Lola moved to a third final window. "'*From the Bhavisyat Mahapuranas'*" she said. "This is the source Haijar cited that is in the London Museum. '*The king asked the holy man who he was. The other replied: 'I am called son of God, minister of the non-believers, relentless in search of the truth. I am Issa.'*'"

Burt squatted and saw that only flimsy wooden ventilation screens denied access to the tombs inside. Sitting on the floor, he kicked the carved panels down. One flew off, bouncing on top of the two crypts below.

"*E stronzata!*" Lola declared, glancing around nervously.

Burt rolled inside. Dust flew out as he dropped to the floor.

Lola stuck her head in the opening he had made. Burt was already trying to lift open the green sarcophagus.

"Are you crazy?" Lola cried.

"This what Bobby was killed for. I'm going to see if it was worth it."

Lola dropped inside beside him.

"Give me a hand, it's stuck." he said.

She made a quick sign of the cross, then placed her hands on top of the cool marble crypt.

"Push together," he told her. "On three. One, two, three."

But the lid wouldn't budge.

"Shove harder."

"I feel sacrilegious."

"Whoever or whatever's in there, I'm going to see!"

"*Certo,*" she said. "For Bobby!"

Throwing her shoulder into it, Lola joined with Burt and slammed against it. The entire lid of the sarcophagus slid off its base, and fell to the floor.

"We wrecked it." Lola cried.

"It doesn't matter. It's open."

Peering inside in the dim rays of the setting sun outside, they saw that it was empty.

"*Vaccagio,*" Lola whispered. "There's nothing here."

Outside, someone cursed in what sounded like Arabic. They looked out to see a man wearing a turban drop to his knees and stick his head through the destroyed ventilation panels. He began shouting furiously at them.

"What's he saying?" Burt wondered.

"Whatever it is, it doesn't sound good." Lola said,

"I think he's mad at us."

The man pointed a rifle at them.

"He's definitely not happy," Burt agreed as they both put their hands up in surrender.

CHAPTER THIRTY—ONE

Querying trains and buses departing New Delhi, a bus company rep had provided passport information of a Burt Powell and Lola Constantino traveling to Srinagar. Since Kashmir was not a member of Interpol, it had taken all morning to process Inspector Jopat's request for a police helicopter into lawless Srinagar. With all the red tape, everything it seemed was necessary to be filled out in triplicate. Finally, after hours of constant phone calls, endless forms faxed, and an insurance agreement signed by the Executive Director in Lyons, everything was at last ready.

By noon, Inspector Rohan Jodpat and his assistant, Muzzafaro were fighting headwinds, dipping under the high peaks of the great Himalayan mountains. The pilot apologized for the rising warm air currents that were unusual for this time of the year. It was small consolation for Muzzafaro, who repeatedly puked into his barf bag.

Radioing ahead, Jodpat alerted the airfield personnel in Srinagar to provide him ground transportation.

***

As *La Ombra* hurried across one of the narrow bridges spanning the fast flowing, muddy brown Jhelum river, she saw to her amazement her pigeons pass by in the back of a jeep. Two turbaned men in *halabas* were holding Kalashnikovs. *La Ombra* watched the vehicle dodge through debris and roar down the street, then slow and turn toward a fenced-off compound. Irregulars in civilian clothes swung the gates open then closed them behind it. The sign above the compound stated: "Srinagar Detention Center."

This changed everything.

Realizing she could not easily break them out of that enclosure, *La Ombra* retraced her steps back to Colonel Bagh in the Border Security Force headquarters at the school. Pushing through the front door, she barged past the same military receptionist with his red cravat and swept through the closed doors into the Colonel's cafeteria office. The receptionist jumped up but remained outside the doors and watched.

Colonel Nasim Bagh looked up as *La Ombra* entered but stayed seated behind his desk set by itself in the middle of the cafeteria.

"Ah," he smiled. "You are back so soon?"

"The criminals I am after were arrested."

He spread his hands to show his innocence. "Not by me or my men."

"True, they did not wear uniforms."

"Then that is not my problem." He frowned. "I fulfilled my end of the bargain."

She said. "But now the two are in a Detention Center."

"They were arrested by Muslims then." He thought a moment. "Perhaps another million rupees."

"You are a thief."

"And you?" he asked. "What are you?"

With disdain, she withdrew a stack of bills, peeled off a million rupees and threw them down on the desk.

The Colonel did not touch them. "I saw how much you have. I want two million. No, make that three."

La Ombra smiled and counted out more from the thick stack. "Here is three million."

The Colonel scooped the huge pile of rupees inside his desk drawer.

"Make the call now," she said. "I want the two freed."

The Lieutenant Colonel smiled and picking up his desk phone, punched a number. He said into the receiver, "This is Colonel Bagh at headquarters. I'm ordering you to release the prisoners someone brought you a few minutes ago."

There was a chatter of protest from the other end that *La Ombra* could not make out.

"I don't care if the Muslim priests brought them there. No, no. These prisoners are not Pashtun. Do they look like Pashtun? Release them immediately or suffer the consequences from the GSF."

La Ombra leaned closer and said. "Have them brought to my helicopter."

"Bring them to the airfield," the Colonel commanded. "Yes, immediately. That is my direct order."

When he replaced the receiver back in its cradle, the Colonel's hand dropped below the desk top, a movement, Delicata observed.

"There," he said. "That's done. But we are not finished."

"No?" *La Ombra* pretended not to notice that he opened a side drawer in his desk.

"I want the rest." He lifted a .45 caliber military weapon.

She fired the hidden Glock held beneath her red nurse's cape. The bullet struck the Colonel in the forehead and he was dead before his head banged down on his desk top.

"So greedy." she commented.

From outside the office doors, the receptionist who had been watching rushed inside. He had seen the whole thing. Now, he saw the nurse riffle through the Colonel's desk, removing what looked like stacks of money.

Carefully, the Corporal withdrew his sidearm. "Put your hands up," he ordered her.

The nurse obeyed, raising her arms. In her right hand, she held a silencer.

"Put down your weapon."

Carefully, she lowered her hand and placed the gun on the desk.

"Now step away from the desk."

This time, instead of obeying him, the nurse simply rolled across the top of the desk and dropped out of sight behind it. He advanced slowly, gun held ready. Once he was near the desk, he pointed his weapon to where she had disappeared. To his confusion, the nurse was not there.

"Turn around," she said.

He realized she had slipped beneath the desk and gotten behind him. But then he saw that her pistol lay still on the desk top. She did not have a weapon.

He spun to shoot her. But was surprised to see she was pointing the Colonel's silver-plated military .45 at him. She shot him in his nose.

Tossing down the Colonel's pistol, Delicata snatched up her silenced Glock, and gathered up the rest of the money. Exiting the cafeteria doors, she pushed through the main entrance and walked toward her waiting chopper.

The guards on duty at the front door saluted her.

CHAPTER THIRTY—TWO

The Detention Center was a concrete bunker with a primitive arrangement of six cells inside. Each had construction rebar with chicken wire stretched across the fronts. Lola and Burt were locked in separate, side by side cells, unable to see one another.

Burt, said, "Are you alright?"

"We came so far. And there was nothing there."

"Something's wrong. Why would Kali risk so much if he knew there were no bones?"

"Maybe he didn't know," Lola offered. "Maybe the tomb has never been opened."

A jailer appeared, keys jangling in his hand. "The crime of desecration against the holy tombs that you committed has serious consequences. The law condemned you to be beheaded."

He opened Lola's iron-barred door. Burt was on his feet instantly.

"Where are you taking her?" he demanded.

Without replying, the jailer next opened Burt's door, then pushed them both forward. "Do not try to run. If you do, you will be shot."

"What if they're going to shoot us anyway?" Lola was trembling as she walked beside him.

The jailer led them through the front door and outside, ordered them to get into the waiting jeep. Two Indian BSF soldiers drove them down the hill, crossing a bridge over the fast-moving river below. Ahead, on the little airfield, Burt saw there was a chopper waiting, its engine already churning its blades, readying for take-off.

Lola said, "I've got a bad feeling about this."

The jeep stopped about a hundred feet from the helicopter and Burt saw the pilot inside gesture to bring them aboard. Rifles rammed into their backs and

Lola and Burt were herded off the jeep, then forced to walk toward the waiting helicopter. Getting closer, Burt was able to see inside the chopper. A nurse in a white uniform, wearing a red cape with the insignia of a slivered moon sat in the rear seat. Her face was obscured.

From the opposite direction, there came the *whomp-whomp* sound of another chopper approaching. As they walked, Burt and Lola saw that helicopter had a blue insignia of a globe with a sword behind it. Beneath it, it said, "International Criminal Police Organization."

"That's Interpol," Lola said. "Oh, *merda!*"

They watched as the chopper set down on a nearby heliport pad.

BSF soldiers prodded them to move faster.

Inside the aircraft they were approaching, Burt saw the nurse at last turn and stare at them, giving at a good look at her bandaged face.

Startled, he whispered to Lola, "When I say, run, run like hell."

She looked at him, not understanding. "Why?"

"Trust me, we get on this chopper, we're dead. Ready?"

"Where do we run to?"

"Head for that Interpol chopper over there."

"To the police? We've been running *from* them, not *to* them."

"Change of plans. Just zig zag."

"*Che testa di cazzo.*" she cursed. "What is a zig zag?"

"Run back and forth, not in a straight line. Now, go!" Burt spun and slugged the closest guard. As he went down, the other one leaped on him.

Alone, Lola broke toward the international police helicopter, running from one side to the other.

Inspector Rohan Jodpat, helping Muzzafaro who was looking green around the gills from the ride, heard a shout. Looking up, he saw a young woman dashing in a broken run toward them. Behind her, a man was fighting two armed Indian paramilitary.

The woman, separated from them by perhaps a hundred yards, kept weaving back and forth, shouting something frantically. In the wash of their chopper's blades, Jodpat couldn't make out what she was saying.

Behind her, the man successfully knocked down the second uniformed soldier and began to race toward the Interpol helicopter. Trying to understand what was happening, Rohan squinted at the scene.

The first BSF paramilitary, recovering from Burt's blow, scrambled to his feet and aimed his Kalashnikov. He fired a burst, sending a spread of slugs exploding behind the fleeing man's legs. The other soldier got up and fired. This time, bullets flew over Jodpat's head.

"Bastard." Rohan ducked.

And then, raising, he recognized the two figures rushing at him.

"It's the fugitives!" he screamed. He drew his Smith-Wesson police Special from his holster and fired it into the air. "Interpol!" he bellowed at the two Indians still shooting.

It did no good. They continued to pop off rounds at the couple as they ran across the landing area. Fortunately, their aims were terrible.

Muzzafaro managed to withdraw his weapon, only to vomit again.

In desperation, Rohan Jodpat ran toward the man and woman, ordering them, "Down. Get down!"

Hearing that, amid a volley of new slugs, Burt pulled Lola down and they collapsed together in a heap on the airstrip.

***

From inside her helicopter, *La Ombra had* watched as the two BSF soldiers herded Burt Powell and Lola Constantino toward her. In a moment, they would be hers. She had been visualizing how to kill them and had come upon a good, simple solution. Once in the air, she would hold her gun on the pilot, and pitch her pigeons out. They would fall together several thousand feet into one of the unreachable, snow-covered morasses of the Himalayas. Their bodies would never be found. After that, she would force the pilot to land somewhere close to civilization and kill him too.

But, as *La Ombra* watched and waited for the two to reach her helicopter, she saw the American sock one of the soldiers.

To make matters worse, the woman bolted away.

Flinging open the side door of the chopper, *La Ombra* put her hand beneath the red cape and grasped the silenced Glock. She swung out, preparing to pursue her quarry and finish them here. But then she saw the woman was running toward a chopper that had just landed. On its side was the white and blue Interpol insignia.

Quickly, she assessed the situation. There were two men outside the Interpol vehicle, two soldiers firing their rifles and two pigeons. It was not impossible to finish her assignment. She had done harder things before.

The pilot inside her own helicopter shouted at her. She glanced back at him. In the wind from the blades, she saw by his frightened expression and waving his hands, that he wanted her to return, so he could depart.

Delicata Fabrizio spun back to the agonizing scene unfolding before her on the airport runway. She saw the Interpol cop fire his gun into the air in warning. The soldiers shooting at her prey. Badly. Then both of her pigeons fall down. Had they been hit? Were they dead?

She could do this! Cooley, she calculated the distance with the number of kills she must make. It was all possible. But then *La Ombra* heard her pilot rev the blades, preparing to take off.

And she realized the problem was she would have no escape. There was no sensible choice but to retreat.

Cursing at being thwarted once again, she forced herself to turn back. In a black mood, she slid inside her chopper and latched the door. As she watched her pigeons rise on the runway and scamper toward the Interpol craft, she felt her pilot lift her away into the Himalayan skies.

CHAPTER THIRTY—THREE

Rome

Just Outside the Vatican Walls

At the time of *La Ombra's* call, it was 6:23 am in Rome and less than a hundred yards across from St. Peter's Square on the Via del Mascherino, Cardinal Montalvo and Monsignor Tuppo were standing as usual at their favorite stainless steel counter espresso bar, drinking their breakfast coffee and munching croissants. Along with early morning businessmen, and other clerics, both met daily in this little hole-in-the-wall called Amado's. It was a favorite gathering place for bishops, cardinals and priests who worked in the Vatican.

As Tuppo took the call from Delicata Fabrizio, the Cardinal surveyed the room, nodding greetings. He was reminded that many of these prelates knew that he headed up the secret brotherhood of the Hand of Christ and condemned his heavy handed tactics. He dismissed them as fuzzy-headed liberals who had no idea of the horrors the real world was capable of.

Locking eyes with his chief antagonist, rail-thin Cardinal Reynaldo Storche, who had openly accused him of not believing the promise Christ made to Peter about the Church's survival when he said, 'You are Peter and upon this Rock I will build my church and the gates of hell shall not prevail against it.' Montalvo had responded that he believed Jesus meant for believers to help fulfill that promise by actively supporting it.

When Monsignor Tuppo signed off with Delicata, the Cardinal smiled at various colleagues and retreated to a small table in the corner where they could speak in private.

"Did she succeed?" the Cardinal impatiently demanded.

Tuppo said, "No, the two fugitives eluded her."

"Where did they go?"

"She believes back to New Delhi, flying with Interpol. That's where she is now, waiting new instructions."

"Another complication."

"Not wishing to waste the trip there to Kashmir, she stayed behind to gather research for us. She reports there is indeed an alleged tomb of Jesus."

"Did she see it?" The Cardinal gripped his demi-tasse cup between both hands and waited. He had been hoping it was all a hoax.

"Yes and she also heard there were tombs of Mary—the Mother of God in a nearby town called Muree and another in Taxbar which belonged to Mary Magdalen."

"Who makes up these wretched stories?"

"Delicata also ascertained from several local Imams that the tomb of Jesus, as it is called, had been opened. They were very upset about that."

"And?"

"She saw the sarcophagus that was supposed to hold the bones of Jesus."

"Yes?"

"It was empty."

"Of course it was!" It took Montalvo a moment to understand. "Nothing inside?"

"Gone. Delicata Fabrizio searched the entire site."

"At least this last item is excellent news. Excellent."

"But what if bones were there? I mean not Jesus's, of course, but somebody they could claim was him. Then what?"

Deep in thought, Montalvo leaned close to Tuppo's ear so no one nearby could hear. "The bones, even if they do exist, no longer matter. All that matters is that the tomb, whoever it belongs to, is without bones. Even if someone has them, their authenticity is gone. The connection has been lost. Wherever they are, they are merely old bones now. They could belong to anyone."

Tuppo smiled, seeing the logic.

"What about the stolen document from our archives?"

"She still has found no trace of it."

"Did you contact the Royal Indian mail service and see if there was any record of where the letter without postage was sent by the heretic priest?"

"They stated it was not within their power to track it. They simply have no such modern methods. They keep no records of such a thing."

"Then the *Yuz Asaf* remains missing. And we do not know where or actually even if a letter was posted."

"For the moment, eminence, no. But if it was sent, we will find it, I assure you."

The Cardinal dusted crumbs off his everyday black cassock with its scarlet piping, adjusted his wide red sash, stood and saw that Cardinal Storche was staring at him. "Anselmo, where will the funeral take place for our fallen brethren, Father Martin Urrutia?"

"Where he taught. Here, at the North American College chapel, Why?"

"Inform the Superior there that I wish to conduct the funeral mass myself. To personally pray for Father Urrutia's soul."

"But he was one of them, a reprobate. A thorn in our side, Eminence."

"Exactly why my presence will be noted by all. My being there will allay rumors that the Hand of Christ had anything to do with Father Urrutia's death."

"Once word gets out you are doing this, the American College chapel will be packed."

As Montalvo departed, he winked at his enemy, Cardinal Storche who looked outraged at the brazen gesture.

CHAPTER THIRTY—FOUR

New Delhi, India

After questioning Burt and Lola, Inspector Jodpat was convinced they had nothing to do with the murders of Father Aloysius in Rome, Wezo the chauffeur, and Father Martin Urrutia in Tarsus, or even the American Air Force Major found dead near Incirlik airport. Additionally, Interpol Inspector Ruben Givas, the Vespery policeman, Officer Tamtam Aroha, along with Nasim Bagh, Lieutenant Colonel and his military secretary in Srinagar had not died at their hands. Counting the Kashmiran that made nine murders total, and, if Burt Powell could be believed about his brother Bobby, it was up to ten. Jodpat knew without a doubt that this was the work of a well-trained, professional killer. And not the two sitting in his office before him.

Putting them onto an Air India plane back to Rome, Inspector Jodpat wished them luck and said he would alert Italian Interpol to aid them any way they could. More he could not do.

But the press had picked up the scent about the multiple murders spread across three countries and Jodpat was forced to hold a press conference. Something he would not ordinarily do under any circumstances. Almost immediately, that information about Burt and Lola leaving for Rome was picked up on the news by the nerds in Lausanne and forwarded to Delicata Fabrizio, who at that very moment, was in New Delhi, trying to figure out where next to pick up the scent of her pigeons.

Learning that they were headed for Rome, she changed costumes, abandoning her nurse's get-up, bought a new outfit of a cowgirl, complete with white Stetson, leather skirt and boots, and booked a flight on Air Italia to Fiumicino airport.

On Air India, during the night flight from New Delhi to Rome, Lola, who had been quiet, finally said to Burt, "Are you awake?"

"I can never sleep on these planes. Anyway, I've been trying to think about our next move. I mean we're at a dead end here. It's all been a wild goose chase. After all this, we're going home empty-handed."

"Maybe not," Lola handed him a mutilated envelope that was covered with notices of "Insufficient Postage," "Return to Sender," "Unable to Return to Sender," "Please Forward," "Collect Postage Due."

"What's this?" Burt turned the wrinkled envelope in his hands.

"Look at the address."

"It's addressed to you."

"To my *appartamento* near the University of Turin. I got it just before leaving to meet you in Rome. Recognize the handwriting?"

Burt studied it but couldn't, "It's barely legible. The writing is so scrawled."

"I didn't recognize the handwriting either." Lola said. "There were no stamps on it. No return address. Cost me six Euros for postage. I had no idea who sent it. Then I noticed that one of the postmarks was from New Delhi."

Burt froze.

"Go ahead, I've already opened it."

Burt lifted the torn and battered envelope's flap. A baggage claim ticket fell out. "Air India Flight 2781 from Indira Gandhi International to Rome, Italy?" he read it.

"It's dated two days before Bobby was murdered."

"So it couldn't have been his. Unless he flew from Turkey to New Delhi then to Rome, and back to Delhi. Which makes no sense at all."

Lola said, "I asked Inspector Jodpat to get hold of the passenger list on the flight. Turns out, that claim ticket belonged to Dr. Izmet Hisban, head of the Archeology Department. "

"The professor from Sringar University? The one Chakri said Kali worked for?"

Lola nodded in agreement. "And that means Dr. Izmet must have flown to Rome sometime before Kali and Bobby met. Because he had to give the claim ticket to Kali so he could hand it to Bobby in New Delhi."

"But why?"

They both stared at the crumpled baggage ticket as if it would give them the answer.

Burt said, "At any rate, Dr. Izmet and Kali clearly did not want its contents known. Except to Bobby."

Lola said, "Maybe it's the *Yuz Asaf?*"

"Maybe. Or maybe something bigger?"

They locked eyes, knowing what each was thinking.

Burt shook his head. "Why didn't you tell me about this before? I mean this whole time you had the envelope from Bobby."

"I told you I didn't know it was from him. . And its contents made no sense. Anyway," she exploded, "I was a little distracted running around, dodging that idiot killer's bullets."

"I'm sorry," Burt smiled. "I had no right questioning you. Forgive me."

He leaned and kissed her, lingering so his lips warmed hers.

"We have to find the checked bag," she said.

"*If* it's still there."

"What do you mean?"

"Airlines sell off or destroy unclaimed luggage after a certain time."

"*Stronzos!*" Lola cursed. "*Cazzo! Testa di cazzo* if they do that!"

The jet's engines dialed back and as the nose lowered for the landing in the Fiumicino airport, a stewardess asked everyone to bring their seats upright and buckle in for the landing.

***

Burt and Lola picked their way through the heavy passenger traffic and spotted the Air India baggage claim window. Inside the booth, a thin, woman with tawny skin, the color of creamed coffee, wore a brown suit with a plastic button on her chest that announced "I Should Never Have Left Morocco". She looked up absently from her "Beano" comic as they arrived.

"*Si?*" she asked without enthusiasm.

"We want to claim some luggage," Lola pushed the ticket under the plastic window. The woman reluctantly put down her comic book, picked up the claim check and stared at it. "This arrived here more than two weeks ago."

"We're running a little late." Lola tried to make a joke.

The Moroccan replied, reverting to a rote message, "First you must see if it is in the baggage room to your right, over there. Then if you do not find it, you must fill out a statement that the luggage is lost."

"And if it is lost?" Burt asked.

"Then the airline will pay you a maximum of $640.00 for the one bag. As I have told you, if it arrived and is still here, you must start by checking the Lost and Found over there for it in that room."

Entering the stuffy, mildew-smelling back room, they saw, to their dismay, that there were hundreds of suitcases, duffel bags, all kinds of luggage, some neatly lined in rows on the floor, others tossed into hasty stacks.

"Let the fun begin." Burt said.

Memorizing the last few numbers on the claim ticket, they divided the room into half and began examining each tag. It took about a half hour for them to complete their task.

"Anything?" Burt asked finally.

She shook her head. "No, and I'm seeing double. Now what?"

"What if Dr. Izmet did not accompany the bag?"

"You mean he never got on the plane? Just bought a ticket and put on the bag?"

"It's possible."

"Not to mention expensive. But doesn't security stop people from doing that?"

"There's always ways," Burt said.

They strode back to the *Bagaglio* window. A woman from Greece was screaming at the Moroccan, berating her for losing her luggage on a flight from London.

"Madam," the officer recited what seemed like a well-worn speech she had memorized. "Heathrow is the largest airport in Europe. We at Leonardo da Vinci are the second largest with thirty-eight million passengers traveling through here every year. Ninety-nine point five percent of the bags arrives okay. That leaves zero point five percent, which means that fifteen thousand bags are mishandled over a year. Usually those are returned to the ticket holder within twenty-four hours. So just three hundred and seventy-eight bags are lost *forever*. Now, I doubt if your luggage is lost *forever*. So, please, take a form, fill it out and bring it back to me. In the meantime, Air India will compensate you twenty-five dollars to replace any incidentals like toiletries."

The woman snatched a form, hurled an invective over her shoulder and strode off.

"This is a job from hell," the Moroccan said to Lola and Burt as they stepped up again to the window.

Burt asked, "What happens to a bag if it's discovered that the ticket holder did not board the same flight?"

She blew out her breath. "If we ascertain the passenger placed luggage on the plane without accompanying it, the bag is seized."

"At departure or arrival?"

"If the computer spots the mismatch early enough, it is confiscated at the flight's origin. If not, then at its destination."

"Then it might still be in New Delhi." Lola said.

"If they spotted it." Burt handed the claim tag to the Moroccan. "Will you check this number on your computer to see if it arrived here?"

"I am not qualified to perform such a task," she picked up her Arabic translated comic book. "I do not have that data."

"Who does?"

"Airport security," she replied, without looking up. "Fourth floor."

***

The moment they left, an India Air pilot in his snazzy blue uniform with gold braids on his shoulders, stepped up to the *Bagaglio* window. The real pilot sat dead in a toilet stall, in a nearby men's restroom, a plastic bag over his head to asphyxiate him. Delicata had chosen that form of death because she did not want any blood on his uniform. The cause of the pilot's demise was simple. He had been *La Ombra*'s size.

"Hello," the blond India Air pilot greeted the Moroccan baggage official. "Having a nice day?"

"Here, it is never a nice day," she said, without looking up from her comic.

"Ah," the pilot gestured at what she was reading. "*Beano*. I love *Beano*. You know '*Tales of Ali Baba and The Forty Thieves?* I just finished reading that comic. I always loved the slave girl Morgana who saves the day. In fact, you remind me of her."

The official looked up then and smiled at the slightly effeminate, yet handsome, pilot.

"What happened to your face?" she asked.

He touched the flesh-colored Curad bandage that hid the butterfly closures beneath. "A little accident."

"Can I help you? Did you lose a bag?" she asked coyly.

"Nothing like that." He looked around. "That couple who was just here? They are my friends. Came in on my flight. I didn't get a chance to say goodbye."

"Ah, those two," she nodded, understanding now. "They lost a bag on a previous flight."

"A previous flight?"

"Yes," she said. "They went up to security to see if it even arrived here." She pointed. "In the Security Room."

The pilot spun in the direction where the couple had gone. "Thank you, princess,"—he touched the bill of his hat and reading her name tag—added, "Qima. Perhaps we will meet again someday."

She sighed as she watched him walk away, then returned to *Beano*.

***

Stepping from the elevator on the fourth floor, Burt and Lola located a sign in the corridor that identified room #412 as "*Sicurezza.*" They walked down that door and pushing inside, came face to face with two Airport Security Guards drinking coffee. Lola spoke Italian with them, showing them the baggage claim check. The guards took the claim check, traded several comments between them, then one unlocked a back door, went into a storage room neatly lined with duffel bags, purses and suitcases on metal shelves.

In a moment, the guard returned, carrying a cheap, gray, plastic Samsonite overnight case. Handing Lola back the claim slip, he told her that because no one had claimed it, the bag had previously been x-rayed for bombs and weapons. But none were found. And now she could fill out a Release Request Form.

She did that and when it was done, the guard handed her the Samsonite case and they left the room.

Out in the hallway, they passed an Air India pilot in uniform. They did not see him watch them as they stepped inside the elevator. In front of the Fiumicino airport's Air India terminal, they boarded a commuter bus that would take them into Rome. Lola sat, holding the Samsonite case flat on her lap.

"Open it." he said. "Let's see what's inside."

"Maybe we should wait. You know, get somewhere we can be careful. Where it's safe."

"It's probably just clothes or something." Burt said, though he did not want to believe that.

"What if it's not?" She glanced around the bus.

For a long moment, Burt stared at her.

Lola saw they were passing an old cemetery. "I can't wait. I know this place. We can be safe here." She stood up and started down the aisle, telling the bus driver to stop.

When he did, they got off the bus and entered a barren field littered with empty plastic bottles, beer and soda cans, newspapers, fast food wrappers. Planes landing at Fiumicino roared overhead as they approached their landings.

Burt asked. "What is this ugly place?"

"A necropolis," Lola said, winding through the broken tombstones. "These burial grounds are over two thousand years old. It was used for slaves."

They walked amidst rows of ancient crumbling grave stones and sarcophagi. Stopping behind a crumbling brick building that was so old it looked like it had melted, Lola squatted and placed the suitcase flat on the ground. "Here goes." she said.

"Wait." Burt was looking at the road they had just come down from. A taxi had stopped and an airline pilot in his uniform jumped out.

"Don't I know him? Who is that?" Lola wondered.

"Whoever it is, it looks like he just followed us here." Burt glanced at the darkened building behind them. "Hide inside."

"It's dark in there. I don't like it."

"I'll be in in a second."

Reluctantly, Lola carried the unopened Samsonite inside, ducking under the low-slung roof, reliving the terror of Mithra's cave. In the dim light, she saw there were hundreds of sarcophagi. She settled behind a large, crumbling crypt, only to have her face covered in spider webs. Forcing herself not to panic, she tore them off.

In a moment, the pilot's silhouette appeared in the archway and raised a gun with a silencer. "I know you're in there. I just heard you. Here I come."

But as he took a step forward, a rock, about the size of a potato, thumped off the back of his head and he collapsed.

Burt tore the weapon from the pilot's hand, then stepped inside the archway and shouted, "You can come out now."

Lola raced toward the welcome daylight and saw the pilot sprawled on the ground. "Is that who I think it is?"

"*La Ombra,* in yet another disguise." Burt said, holding her Glock.

"Now I know where I remembered the pilot. He passed us in the hallway outside the Security office. It's her alright Look, she's still got a big Band-Aid on her face," Lola said. "Why didn't I notice that?"

"Because you're stupid," *La Ombra* jumped up and jerking a small caliber pistol from inside her jacket, aimed it at Lola.

Burt shot her twice, pointblank. The slugs drove the wind out of her and the assassin dropped her weapon as she fell out of sight behind a sarcophagus.

Gun raised, Burt inched forward. But when he swung around the tomb, she was gone.

"She's alive!" he couldn't believe it. "I hit her. I should have killed her!" Hurriedly, Burt prowled forward, ready to shoot.

Stumbling away amidst the standing tomb stones, her ribs feeling like they were broken, *La Ombra* slipped off the pilot's blue jacket, removed the black tie, then the white shirt to reveal a bullet proof Kevlar vest beneath that she always wore. Undoing its Velcro straps, she peered at the two large reddish blue bruises where the slugs had hit her chest. Hopping, she eased off the pilot's black shoes and socks, stepping lastly out of the blue trousers.

As a jet rumbled low overhead, Delicata, barefoot, clad now only in her black Victoria Secret bra and panties, saw Burt appear behind her. When he looked at her, he decided it was not his prey and turned away in another direction.

Turning the pilot's blue jacket inside out so its white silk lining showed, she tied its arms together into a loop. then hung it fashionably over one shoulder so it resembled a carry bag. Casually, she strolled long- legged, out of the necropolis. Disguised now as a vacationer, she picked her way barefoot toward the nearby lakeside resort of *Casceina Madonna degli Olmi*.

As she sauntered past several *carabinieri* in a passing car, the sexy killer smiled at them.

A wolf whistle from one of the horn dog Italian cops made her day.

CHAPTER THIRTY—FIVE

They fled the ruins of the necropolis and flagged down a taxi driver who drove them into Rome.

"Where to?" the cabbie asked.

"The best hotel in Rome," Lola said. "I want a bath. And good clean sheets too."

"You heard the lady," Burt said.

The driver dropped them off at the Hassler hotel and they splurged on an eight hundred dollars per night room that overlooked the Spanish Steps. Once in their room, Lola said, "Alright, we've put this off long enough. Time to see what's inside the suitcase." Laying the Samsonite case on the big bed, she snapped open the two metal latches and lifted the lid.

In their fourth floor luxurious room, with the twinkling lights of the city coming on below, Lola and Burt stared in shock at the contents. Tenderly, she reached inside and lifted out a yellowed human skull. A tremor ran through her as she realized the import of who she might be holding.

Burt lifted out several small bones, the connective tissue long gone. "Fingers?" he wondered.

There were two long bones, each about ten inches. "Upper arms. So old, yet in perfect condition."

"Is this a wrist?"

Lola spotted tiny gouges between the bones. "Where they drove the nails, fixing him to the cross?"

"This could be the most precious relic of all Christendom."

"Or its downfall."

Both of them stared at the trove, letting the meaning of what they had sink in.

"Maybe they're not real," Burt offered. "Maybe they're just bones belonging to someone else named Jesus."

"There you go with maybes again."

"What do we do with them?"

"What do you want to do?"

"If the world learns about these bones, then what?"

"Well, most Christians would never believe they belong to Jesus. They couldn't afford to."

"And the church will want them destroyed."

"Certainly the Hand of Christ would."

"Look," Burt said. "Maybe we should just forget the whole thing. You know, dump them in the ocean or something. Get rid of them. Make them disappear forever. It would solve everything for everybody. Any way you look at it, they're nothing but trouble. Besides, like I said, we don't even know for sure they belong to Jesus."

"And we don't know for sure they don't." Lola studied him. "I wonder what Bobby would have done."

"He would have hidden them until he knew their authenticity. I mean he would never destroy them without knowing. And even then."

"But where?"

"I have no idea," Lola said. "And anyway I want a bubble bath. Maybe I'll come up with something brilliant."

While Lola took a bath, Burt put a call through to Inspector Jodpat in Delhi. There was a time difference of five hours, but he caught the Interpol officer as he arrived early for work.

"Rohan," Burt said, after amenities, "has Chakri, his wife, claimed the body of Kali Mohi from the morgue yet?"

"Hold on," he said. "I'll check." There was a minute's delay, then he came back on. "The body is still there. But his wife has notified the morgue that she arrives today to take him for burial. What are we speaking of here, Officer Powell?"

"The same assassin who killed my brother, tried to murder us here in Rome. I was able to get her gun. My fingerprints are on it because I shot her."

"Did you kill her?"

"I think she was wearing a vest."

"Too bad. But you think you have the same murder weapon she used here in Delhi to kill Mr. Mohi?"

"It's a long shot, but all we've got."

"If this is true, she has left a long chain of evidence. A most unusual weakness for a professional assassin. Usually they get rid of their weapon after using it."

Burt held his breath. "So, here's my question. Was there an autopsy performed on Kali? If so, was a slug found inside him?"

"I see where you are going with this. If Kali's got a bullet still inside him, we can hopefully match it to the killer."

"This same weapon might also have killed my brother Bobby. I did find what looked like a 9 mm hole in his skull. His death would be reclassified a homicide. And that would mean he did not take his own life."

There was a moment's silence. Then Rohan said, "I am going to recommend to the New Delhi police that they hold Kali's body and perform the autopsy."

"Will they listen to you?"

"Maybe. You realize, as Interpol, I only have powers to recommend. I cannot command. However, I will push hard."

"His poor wife." Burt said. "I hope Chakri will understand."

"I'll contact her personally and explain." Inspector Jodpat said. "If we do find a spent bullet inside Kali, I will need it to verify the ballistics to the gun."

"How do I get the weapon to you?"

"Send it by DHL. Interpol has an account with them that Indian Customs allows through. I will have someone from Interpol in Rome, drop off a pre-addressed box to wherever you are staying."

"We're at the Hassler."

"I hope you have a big credit card," Jodpat laughed. "Ship the gun to me and keep your fingers crossed. Now I must hurry and intercept Kali's body before it is released."

As Burt hung up, Lola emerged from her bathroom, wrapped in a white silk robe, provided by the hotel. He thought she looked beautiful.

She came into his arms and kissed him. "Come up with where to hide the bones?"

"I was distracted, thinking of other things," she kissed him again.

A beam of light flashed back and forth across both of them.

Burt broke off and looked where it was coming from.

"What is that?" Lola looked disappointed. "It's nothing. Just someone playing around."

Moving to the window, Burt stared down at a streetlight below on the *Via di San Sebastianello.* A man was standing beside a pile of cobblestones that workers had left there while performing street repair. He raised a flashlight again and swept it across the window Burt was standing at.

Lola came by his side and saw that the figure was swathed in a black overcoat. "Who is he?"

"Or she?"

"Stay here."

"You're going down there? Holy Sponge!"

"If it looks like I'm in trouble, call the cops." He pocketed *La Ombra*'s silenced Glock. "No, better idea, don't call them. Just run! "

"Where do I go?"

Burt said, "To the Spanish steps below. I'll find you."

As Lola watched, he crept out of the room. In a few minutes, she spotted him down the street, crossing, dodging several cars. He circled around beneath the trees and when he was behind the figure lunged and wrapped his arm around the figure's throat.

"Friend, friend!" the black coated man managed. "I'm Father Tom Wheeler. Bobby's friend."

Burt spun him around. In the street light, he saw the Roman Collar and a young priest's face. "Sorry, I thought you were that bitch again. What are you doing here?"

"I came to warn you," Father Wheeler tried to catch his breath.

"About what?"

"I believe they already know where you're staying. I didn't dare come inside the hotel. I used this flashlight to get your attention, hoping you would come down here."

Burt said, "How did you know we were here?"

"Like the Hand of Christ, we have our own organization, our own intelligence. You were not too smart to take out a room here with your credit card."

Burt stood before him. "I guess we were both tired of running."

"Understandable," the priest said. "But careless."

Burt pulled the priest away from the light, back into the shadows of the trees along the street. "If you're right, we've got to move."

"Where will you go?"

Burt glanced around. "To a park, somewhere, anywhere they can't track us, it doesn't matter."

"This is why I came. You must come with me, to the American College. You can take Bobby's old room tonight. It's still vacant."

Burt pulled away. "I'll get our stuff and be down as soon as we can."

"I'll wait here," Father Wheeler said. "I have a car. Oh, there is something else. Cardinal Montalvo will say a Mass for Father Urrutia tomorrow at the College."

"So, who's Montalvo?"

"The big cheese, the boss who runs the Hand of Christ."

Burt stepped close to Father Wheeler. "The one who ordered my brother's death?"

"The very same." In the meager light, he saw the American grin wolfishly.

"Then I'll look forward to meeting him."

"Why?"

"So someday I will know what he looks like."

The priest watched anxiously as Burt retraced his steps across the street to the Hassler.

***

After leaving the Hassler, Father Wheeler drove Burt and Lola to the North American College campus. He showed Lola to a vacant room, then took Burt to Bobby's. Bidding him good night, Burt placed the suitcase with the bones on Bobby's bed. They had decided not to tell Father Wheeler about its contents.

He surveyed his brother's spare, monk-like room. A little beat-up desk faced the window, an old straight backed chair, narrow, single bed. Sitting at the desk, Burt noticed a holy card scotch taped on the computer monitor, depicting the Shroud of Turin. Beside the desk, there was an unattached electrical cord and several disconnected cables. Had someone taken Bobby's computer? He peeked into the waste basket. It had been emptied.

Standing, Burt crossed over to Bobby's book shelves. Lots of scholarly works, in Greek, Coptic, Arabic, Italian, Latin. It reminded him how educated his brother was. Bachelor's in Philosophy, Doctorate in Theology, a Ph.D. in Early Christian studies, his long history of publishing papers in scholarly journals on esoteric themes. Some of which he had sent him. What were they about? He couldn't remember because he'd never read any of them.

A photo on a shelf caught his eye. It was of Bobby and himself eight years ago, celebrating Thanksgiving in Ebbetsburg, both of their arms draped over each other's shoulders, wearing orange colored t-shirts that said "Wild Turkeys!" Even in this ridiculous get-up, his twin brother, though grinning, somehow looked different. Way back when he was a little kid, Bobby had somehow seemed purposeful.

On the nightstand beside the bed, he found Bobby's daily breviary. Picking it up, he saw that the black leather covers were worn from use. He knew that despite his scientific and inquisitive mind, Bobby was very devoted to the faith. More than he could say for himself. Idly, Burt leafed through the various sections of the breviary: Vespers, Lauds, Matins.

He put down the book and crossed to the bathroom, which was in immaculate shape. Using the toilet, he flushed it, but had to wiggle the handle several times to shut off the water flow. It crossed his mind that Bobby would have fixed that. He started to lift the lid to see if there was a problem, when there was a quiet knock on the door.

He opened it and Lola entered. "I have a room down the hallway. But I am lonely." She sat beside the Samsonite suitcase with the bones on the bed and said, "I like being here. His scent is in this room. Father Bobby wore Old Spice Swagger."

"Nothing subtle about Bobby," Burt said

"Well he didn't have to please a woman, did he?" She pushed him down on the bed and knelt over his chest, straddling him.

"This feels wrong."

"Yes," Lola smiled. "I like it."

And she began undressing him.

CHAPTER THIRTY—SIX

Rome

North American College

Chapel

On the Janiculum hill that overlooked Vatican City, inside the modern Pontifical North American College, founded by American bishops and dedicated to America's first saint, Mother Cabrini, the chapel's pews were packed with seminarians in black cassocks who had been Father Urrutia's and Father Bobby Powell's devoted pupils. Led by Cardinal Giuseppe Montalvo and Monsignor Anselmo Tuppo, along with Urrutia's professorial colleagues also in Mass vestments, the celebrants surrounded the altar, saying a funeral High Mass for Urrutia whose casket stood just outside the sanctuary. Father Powell, whose death was declared a suicide, would receive no such honor.

Because he was a priest, Father Urrutia was positioned with his head toward the altar but his copper coffin had been ordered closed because of his massive head wounds. The choir sang *a cappella* in the choir loft, chanting the ancient Gregorian dirge of *"Dies Irae, Dies Illa"*, the prayer that begged mercy and forgiveness for the departed soul who was now standing before the throne of God.

Side by side, Burt and Lola, wearing newly-bought dark suits, sat boldly in the front row, only feet from the casket. Cardinal Montalvo and Tuppo, who had seen photos of them. startled at the sight. Containing himself, the Cardinal finished his sacred tasks, then returned to his *sedis,* a throne-like chair, behind the altar. There, sitting next to Tuppo, he grimly eyed Burt and Lola.

"What audacity. Have they no respect for anything?" he whispered. "Where is Delicata?"

"She is here," Tuppo said. "She wanted to pray for Urrutia's soul."

"Then we finish it," Montalvo hissed.

After the chant finished, silence descended upon the chapel and the priests and seminarians bowed their heads to pray for the dead. To Lola's surprise, Burt stood up. She watched as all eyes followed him past the casket then into the sanctuary as he mounted the steps of the pulpit.

In shock, the Cardinal watched the man who was his enemy, ascend the sacred podium then face the faithful.

"Get him down from there," Montalvo ordered.

Monsignor Tuppo angrily stood to remove him.

Burt thumped the microphone with his finger. Hearing it was live, its sound magnified across the chapel, he said, "I'm Burt Powell, Father Bobby's brother. And I have a few things I'd like to say. I know some of you here were Father Bobby's students, his friends and colleagues."

The American seminarians straightened to attention as Burt's strong voice cut across the chapel.

"You!" Tuppo stood at the bottom of the pulpit's steps. "Stop this instantly. You have no right being there."

"I have every right," Burt said. "Now go sit down and wait until I'm done. If you don't, I'll tell everybody how you had my brother and a lot of other good people killed."

"I what?" Anselmo tried to speak. "How dare you insinuate such a thing!"

"Call the police, please, Monsignor," the Cardinal ordered in a flat voice.

Immediately, Tuppo hustled away from the altar and entering the sacristy, pulled out his cell phone.

Burt turned back to the stunned congregation. "Now where was I? Oh, yeah, what I was about to say was you all know that Bobby was a fearless researcher, never afraid to pursue the truth wherever it led. No matter the cost. And as many of you also know, he paid a heavy price doing it. Some think he killed himself. But I know differently. And believe me it will all come out who murdered him."

Smiling proudly, Lola said in admiration, "*Che palle!* What balls!"

"Over the past few days," Burt continued, "in trying to find out what Bobby was seeking as well as prove that he did not commit suicide, I learned some life-changing lessons."

Tuppo re-entered and took his seat beside the Cardinal. "The police are on their way."

"I learned," Burt spoke with passion to the young candidates for priesthood whose faces were raised up to him in the pulpit. "I learned that there are men in the church who use assassinations, who will do anything, because they are afraid of the truth. And I also discovered that my brother understood that the only thing of value in the world is the truth."

There was an uneasy shifting in the congregation.

The Cardinal muttered loudly, *'Basta."*

Ignoring him, Burt unfolded a piece of paper. "I found this behind a book in Bobby's room. It's from the Gospel of St. Thomas, written while Jesus was still alive. Way before Matthew, Mark, Luke or John's gospels. Thomas's gospel was condemned as not fitting the correct truth dictated by the church. St. Thomas writes, 'And Jesus said, if you bring forth what is within you, what you bring forth will save you. If you do not bring forth what is within you, what you do not bring forth will destroy you.'"

Burt folded the paper. "I think Thomas was talking about telling what he knew. Telling the truth. Not building something on lies."

From the back of the church, two *carabinieri* in blue uniforms burst through the doors. Guns strapped to their white belts, boots thudding the floor, they marched up the main aisle. Seminarians and priests all gaped as they hurried toward the altar.

"At last!" Montalvo said.

"There!" Monsignor Tuppo stood and pointed at Burt in the pulpit. "Arrest him!"

Burt did not resist as the police led him down. As he passed her in the aisle, Lola took his hand and joined him, marching beside him. A few seminarians and priests stood and applauded. But most studiously looked away, ignoring them as they passed.

In the last row, her short black hair still dyed blond, *La Ombra*, dressed as a seminarian in cassock and collar, watched as Burt was taken by the *carabinieri* through the back doors. In a moment, she genuflected and followed.

Outside the Mother Cabrini chapel, the two policemen handcuffed Burt. A priest emerged from the chapel doors and said, "I'm Father Tom Wheeler, Rector of this North American College. What's the charge, officers?"

"We were called by Monsignor Anselmo," one said, "this man was disturbing the ceremony."

"And don't forget trespassing."

"He was not trespassing. Take off the cuffs and go away," he ordered them. "No one is going to press charges."

They looked at each other. "But it is in our report we must make. We were called here."

"I will be down tomorrow at the precinct to give you my full statement about this. It is all a mistake and a misunderstanding."

Again, they conferred. One said to Burt. "You will come down to the station too?"

"I'm a police officer in the United States. You have my word on that."

They nodded, satisfied, got back in their squad car and drove away.

Father Wheeler said, "You put on quite a show in there. I believe that was a first time the gospel of St. Thomas has ever before been read from a pulpit."

"And probably won't ever be again," Lola said.

Burt said to Lola, "Did you see *La Ombra*?"

"No! Is she here?"

"Yeah, as a blond seminarian."

"Then she knows we're here too. We have to go."

"No, the running is over. Now we turn the tables."

CHAPTER THIRTY—SEVEN

They hid in a breezeway that ran between the American College's classrooms, watching from behind Roman columns as the funeral congregation with Father Urrutia's casket, entered the cemetery below. They did not see *La Ombra* in the entourage. In about an hour, when the ceremony was finished and all had left, only then did Burt and Lola walk down the little knoll toward Father Martin Urrutia's open grave.

Two gravediggers appeared driving a tractor. They alighted with shovels, preparing to lower the coffin that hung over the grave and fill it with dirt. As they approached, Burt checked carefully around the area, then said to Lola, "Tell them, we need a moment alone."

She nodded, went over to the two old men, both in gray overalls, who said this was the last grave of the day and after this one they were finished. Lola talked to them in Italian, asking if they would take a coffee break, or perhaps some vino, then handed them some Euros. "We came late and want to say our goodbyes." They looked at each other and one said, of course, they would be back in a half hour or so.

Burt and Lola waited until the gravediggers drove the little tractor over the rise.

"We didn't see her here at the grave. You think she's here?"

"Yeah, I'd bet on it. She's watching our every move." Burt stepped to the coffin which was held over the hole by ropes attached to a winch. He jammed his fingers beneath the top lid, and pulled up. It wouldn't budge.

"It must be sealed," Lola guessed.

Grabbing one of the shovels the grave diggers had left, she jammed its blade under the lid, then levered it up. With a whoosh of air escaping its vacuum, the casket's top popped up a crack.

Flipping it all the way open, Burt could see Father Urrutia laid out in his black priestly suit, wearing a white roman collar. His eyelids were closed, but the sockets were sunken. The bullet holes in his face and throat, though hidden by wax and pancake make-up, were still very visible.

"He wouldn't have liked to be buried in black," Lola said. "Thought it was boring." Her eyes brimmed with tears at seeing his terrible wounds. She reached inside and smoothed his hair back "Goodbye, *maestro.*"

Placing the envelope Bobby had sent from India in Urrutia's hands, Burt lowered the lid and closed it. Manning the hand winch, he twirled the little metal wheel, lowering the casket down into the open grave.

When it had settled entirely at the bottom of the six-foot hole, Burt put his arm around Lola and together they walked away.

***

La Ombra stood above the cemetery behind the American College chapel, overlooking St. Peter's basilica below. From her viewpoint, she had kept track of Burt and Lola all day and now saw them go down to Urrutia's grave send away the grave diggers. Puzzled, she then saw the touching little ceremony performed by the two as they placed an envelope inside the coffin. What was in it? By the looks of its tattered condition, she wondered if perhaps it was the envelope the priest had mailed that day in New Delhi before she shot him. Perhaps it even held the *Yuz Asaf* document itself. If so, with its retrieval, a major part of her contract would be completed. And killing these two pigeons today would free her to return home to the arms of Massimo.

Last night, her nerds in Lausanne had alerted her that the two had used a credit card and checked into the Hassler hotel. But she was too late arriving there. The room was empty. Now was her chance. It would take only seconds to get the document, and then kill the two idiot pigeons.

Quickly, she scanned the little rolling hills. Heavy oak trees populated its hillsides, the light in the sky was dimming, and the cemetery not easily viewed from the street or by any witnesses from any angle. Satisfied there was no one in sight, in her latest disguise wearing a seminarian's cassock, the assassin walked down and paused behind a huge towering oak, again checking to make sure her prey was leaving. Yes, a mere hundred yards away, their backs to her. Perhaps, she reconsidered her plan, she should kill them first. But no, she had no silencer on her back-up gun. Shooting the pigeons would attract attention with the noise. She must secure the document first, then attack. She visualized herself grabbing the document and sprinting toward them, killing them both. She noted carefully that two shovels were stuck in the pile of dirt waiting to be thrown down upon the casket, waiting for the return of the grave keepers. She had only seconds now.

With a bound, Delicata Fabrizio raced to the grave site.

Withdrawing her back-up weapon, a Military semi-automatic, she leaped down onto the top of the copper metal casket, her feet making a loud thud as she landed. Quickly, she placed the M1911 .45 down, then jammed her fingers under the top half of the lid and lifted.

The fat priest held the envelope with its many postmarks in his hands. She snatched it from his grasp and ripped it open. Inside, there was nothing.

Realizing she had been tricked, she shrieked and crumpled the envelope.

A movement behind her made her lunge for the pistol, but before she could grab it, the sharp edge of a shovel opened the top of her skull, exposing her brain. Half dead she instinctively again reached for her weapon. Burt drove the shovel's blade down again, this time into the side of her face, severing off her nose. The assassin fell, mortally stricken, collapsing on top of Urrutia's open casket.

Lola ran up beside Burt and stared down into the grave. *La Ombra* lay sprawled half in, half out of the copper casket, her blood seeping in rivulets across Urrutia.

Lola jumped down and shoved the killer off him. She closed the casket, and apologized, "*Mi perdone, padre.*"

The killer's body had wedged itself between the earth and the side wall of the coffin. Burt threw in the first shovelful of dirt on her.

"*Porca puttana.*" Lola grabbed the other shovel, and began tossing soil.

Together, they piled earth into the hole, covering the casket and the killer. It took about fifteen minutes of hard labor to fill the entire grave.

As they finished, the two gravediggers returned, chugging their tractor over the little rise.

"Do you think they saw anything?"

"We'll soon find out."

Seeing the grave had been filled. the two old men in cemetery overalls slowed in amazement.

They got off and one of them asked Lola something in Italian.

"He wants to know why we did their job?"

"Tell him," Burt was sweating. "To honor our brother."

Lola repeated that.

The men looked at one another, then nodded with respect.

"*Va a Dio.*" one told them.

"*Ottimo lavoro,*" the other waved as Burt and Lola walked up the hill.

"What did they say?" Burt asked.

"Go with God." Lola translated. "The other one gave us a compliment. He said, 'Good job.'"

Looking back from the little rise, they saw the diggers stomping dirt clods on top of the grave, leveling it, smoothing the earth.

Burt put his arm around Lola.

"It's over," she said.

"Maybe not."

"There you go again with maybe."

"Someone has to fess up about what happened to Bobby. Until then it's not over."

CHAPTER THIRTY—EIGHT

Arriving for his meeting with Pope Leo XIV in his long black limousine, Indian Ambassador Tiano Nadi was driven through the Gate of St. Anne, past the Swiss Guard station there, and taken directly to the *Piazza Della Governatorato*, and the Government Palace it overlooked. Because the Ambassador had been crippled as a child with polio, he was forced to use metal crutches. The Holy Father, learning this, chose to greet his visitor as he emerged from his car, an unusual arrangement, opposed by the Swiss Guard. Once they had embraced, knowing that every building, including the Civil Administration Building was full of staircases and many steps, all without elevators, Pope Leo XIV had arranged for them to sit in the pleasant Vatican gardens behind the Church of St. Stephen.

As Ambassador Nadi's black Mercedes appeared, the Holy Father emerged from the Palace and opened his arms in greeting. In a blinding flash, the sunny day erupted into brighter light as a fireball blew apart the limousine. Its steel roof peeled off, shooting high into the air, followed by the skyrocketing body of the Ambassador and his crutches. The two Swiss Guards accompanying the Pontiff were killed by the blast, their bodies shattered. The Holy Father, lifted off his feet, was flung back hard against the steps of the Government Palace.

From inside the Vatican Library, Cardinal Giuseppe Montalvo and Monsignor Anselmo Tuppo watched below as fireman arrived to douse the fierce blaze. Ambulances bore away the corpses of the Ambassador and Pope Leo XIV.

"There will be conjecture," Tuppo said. "Many conspiracy theories."

"As there were before," Montalvo agreed. He was referring to that short 33-day reign of Pope John Paul I who perished in September 1978, allegedly dying of a heart attack. His death had come one day after he announced he would liberalize the Vatican.

"Eighteen popes have been allegedly poisoned, stabbed, suffocated and strangled throughout the long history of the papacy." Anselmo recited.

"You know your history."

"That's my job, *Eminencia.*"

"Pope Leo was on the wrong side. He knew it. We warned him but he wouldn't listen. All that talk about Hindus joining us in the next Vatican Council."

"Along with Buddhists, Shintos, Jews, Islamists and even atheistic Communists participating. What was he thinking?"

"Whatever he had in mind is a thing of past now."

"I heard someone told Leo about the false tomb and that Ambassador Nadi may have invited him to visit it."

'*Infamia!* Even Leo would not have been so stupid as to authenticate its heretical existence."

Massimo, *La Ombra*'s brother and fellow assassin in the Fabrizio clan, stood silently behind them. "My work is done. I should go, *Eminencia.*"

Montalvo rose and embraced him heartily. "Give my respect to your father, my old friend, Umberto. I will not forget this favor."

Massimo said sorrowfully. "It is the least my family could do."

"Have you heard anything more?"

We've lost contact with Delicata. There is a weak signal our people in Lausanne are trying to trace but no luck so far. It appears she is dead and has failed in her duty."

"Will you avenge her?"

"The Delicata family never seeks revenge. It is a waste of time. We work only for money. It is a hard rule taught by my father that if you are killed doing your job, then you have no one to blame but yourself."

"We will need you to fulfill her contract," the Cardinal said.

"I am at your service," Massimo bent his knee and kissed the prelate's huge ruby ring.

CHAPTER THIRTY—NINE

Newspapers, radio and TV carried the Pope's assassination story worldwide. Speculation on who was responsible ran from Islamic fanatics to Christian right wingers to Chinese Communists. Newspapers and tabloids had a field day with photos, opposing editorials, all pinning the cause of such a terrible tragedy ultimately on various groups. In Rome and all of Italy, the police were stretched thin, attempting to calm people, convince them they were safe and make sense of such a tragedy. To complicate matters, the Vatican, as usual, dragged its heels and generally refused to cooperate or divulge any information.

Over coffee the morning after the pope's murder, Father Tom Wheeler, Burt and Lola sat in the college cafeteria reading The Local, an English digital newspaper on a laptop.

"They're getting bolder," Wheeler said.

"If it is the Hand of Christ," Burt said.

"It is," Lola said. "They hated Pope Leo making peace with religions. They said it made the church equal to them."

Wheeler agreed. "We have been hearing threats that they were thinking of doing this. We even heard rumors they wanted to put up Cardinal Montalvo as the next Holy Father. But I doubt he would have been elected. I never thought they would go this far." He paused. "They're very determined. They won't give up on you either, you know. They'll come for you both again."

"The bitch is dead," Burt said.

"They'll send somebody else. You should both get out of Italy while there is still time."

"I made a deal to show up at the police station today," Burt said. "I keep my word."

"You go there," Father Wheeler said, "and they will arrest you and then something will happen in a cell. An accident."

"He's right," Lola locked eyes with Burt. "The Hand of Christ are everywhere."

Father Wheeler excused himself. He had a theology class to lecture, so Burt and Lola had another coffee.

"We have to move the bones," Lola whispered softly even though the cafeteria had emptied.

Both knew the bones were in danger of being discovered. Hidden in Father Bobby's room at the moment, the lack of security was an open invitation to the Hand of Christ.

"I think you should take them somewhere." Burt said.

"Where? I know. Maybe I'll put them in St. Peter's basilica, inside a wall or something. Or in the necropolis beneath the main altar. That would be an interesting place."

"Wherever it is," Burt said, "it should be both outside Italy and fitting."

"Fitting?"

"Some place that has meaning."

Lola sipped her espresso. "Like where?"

"You'll think of something. For the time being, you could stay in my house in Ebbetsburg. The bones will be safe there. So will you."

"What will you do?"

"I'll follow in a while."

Borrowing a car from Father Wheeler, Burt drove Lola from the American College to the nearby seaport of *Ostia Antica*. There, with arrangements already in place, thanks to Father Wheeler, who promised to also ship Bobby's body back to the States, Burt walked Lola down to the docks and the freighter *Bona Natalia*, waiting to depart. The plan was for Lola to sail to Genoa, then take a train to Milan where she could board a flight to the United States. She carried a soft bag and the Samsonite suitcase of bones.

"Why not just come now with me?" she held him tight.

He grinned and said, "Hey, I'm just going down to the corner store to buy a pack of gum."

She realized what he was saying and the import that he had spoken those words to her.

"What flavor?" She fought back tears.

"Juicy Fruit." he said.

CHAPTER FORTY

The clock beside the bed in his cheap rented room showed "2:07 am." Time to move.

Burt had had a dream during the night of a man digging up Father Urrutia's grave. It had been Monsignor Tuppo. He was already deep down inside the hole and had found the top of the metal casket when a woman's foot popped out of the dirt. The monsignor dropped to his knees and screamed something. Scrabbling away earth, unearthed her leg, and pulled and out came the assassin, caked with dirt and blood.

And that is when Burt awakened. He lay there in the darkness, breathing hard, hearing the monsignor's vengeful screams.

Quietly, he slid out of bed and went into the bathroom. Dressing in Bobby's priestly black pants, black jacket and white collar, and black rubber-soled shoes he had found in his brother's room, he went downstairs to the empty lobby, then out through the motel's front door. Outside, the streets were still dark, the orange street night lamps glowing.

Because it was close to the Vatican, he had deliberately taken a room in this run-down motel in the Jewish district called the *Trastevere,*. Recalling the map Father Wheeler had given him, Burt ran along the street called *Lungotevere della Farnesina.* that followed the dried up Tiber river. At the intersection of *Via Santo Spirito,* he turned to a large three story, square-shaped ancient brick building that he knew was the Palace of the Holy Office.

Burt had learned that Cardinal Montalvo slept in a room on the top floor called "Palace of the Arch-Priest. How fitting this was for Cardinal Montalvo.

Using the nylon climbing rope he had bought, he threw its attached metal hook up at the top metal balcony railing. He had not been able to find a proper grappling hook but had used an old broken iron cross he found at the college. When the cross snagged on the balcony, it was a simple matter to haul himself up to the top floor. Compared to what he had done in the war, scaling and entering buildings while the enemy slept inside, this was a piece of cake.

Gaining the balcony, he swung over the railing. The large ten-foot-tall windows were closed and locked. A second balcony to the room was less than ten feet away. Silently, Burt stood on the railing and leaped across. To his relief, a large window stood open.

Stepping into the room, Burt crossed to the bed where a sleeping figure lay. In the light from the street below, he could just make out that it was the Cardinal.

Something, a premonition perhaps, woke Montalvo from his slumber. He opened his eyes but did not see the shadow standing beside his bed. And he did not hear a hand swoop down on him like some great bird claw clamping his mouth. He reached quickly beneath his pillow and found the derringer.

Before he could raise it, though, Burt bent his wrist forward and took it away.

He said to Montalvo, "If you lie, if you do not answer me truthfully every question I ask, you are dead. I will kill you immediately, do you understand?"

Montalvo froze, concentrating totally on the sharp tip of a blade held at his throat.

"Now tell me, how did Father Bobby Powell really die."

"Oh, my, you again?" Montalvo cried out, understanding now who his assailant was. "What is so important that you continue doing this?"

"Something you wouldn't understand."

"Tell me. I will try. I promise."

"You not only took my brother's life, you took every possibility of who he was meant to become. To assassinate his character and honor as a priest, you told the world he committed suicide. You stripped him of all his dignity and worth then had your killer hang him on a bridge to rot."

"I didn't do that. It was her." The Cardinal felt the pressure of the blade's point increase against his skin."Funny, I don't believe you."

Montalvo croaked, "May I get up? I am sleeping naked. I want to get some clothes on. I feel..."

"Like you are powerless?"

"You can't do this! I'm a Cardinal. Do you know how powerful I am?"

The knife sliced through the first layer of skin and drew blood. "What makes you believe you are above the law?"

"Ow, ow please, please." Montalvo tried to wriggle away. "Do you really think this is what your brother would have wished you to do? To hurt me like this?"

"You got it all wrong, big shot," Burt said, pinning him again. "I don't do this for Bobby. I'm doing it for me."

"But, but you're a policeman, are you not? Your job is to obey the law. To do your duty. To protect! Not hurt!"

Burt leaned close, "I was also a soldier who was taught there are enemy who do not deserve the civilized benefit of the law."

"Then you, you're a bad cop! A horrible man!"

"I can live with it. Can you? Like an old farmer once told me, it's like the donkey saying to the rabbit, 'Ain't you got big ears'?"

"I don't know what you are saying."

"Alright I'll come to the point. I'm saying you are evil and do not deserve to live."

Montalvo, realizing his intentions, made a keening sound of desperation. Groaning in terror, he panicked and tried to sit up. Burt slammed him back down flat on the bed.

"Last chance. And if you don't answer, I'm going to assume you're guilty. Did you give the orders to have Bobby killed?"

"Me?" the churchman whined, trembling. "I'm, I'm a Cardinal..."

The knife sliced deep, so blood swelled up in the wound and flowed. Montalvo could feel it running down his chest. "You're killing me."

"You lied."

Montalvo yelped. "Alright, yes, he was killed by an assassin."

"Your assassin and at your orders."

"Yes, yes, what does it matter? Your brother was an enemy. You can understand that. You said so yourself."

"Who did it for you? Was it that costume dresser who murdered Father Urrutia too?"

"Her name was Delicata Fabrizio. She is part of a family of killers we use. But now she has disappeared!"

"Gone forever."

"You killed her?" Montalvo asked.

"Buried her too."

"*Santa Maria!*"

"Is it true she also killed Kali, the Indian from Kashmir, and that Interpol Inspector on the flight to Delhi?"

"I swear I don't know all of the victims you are mentioning. There is always collateral damage in these contracts, you understand?"

"Better than you do, Cardinal Giuseppe Montalvo." He pushed the knife into his throat.

The prelate screamed or tried to.

"Shh," Burt said, "you'll wake somebody up. The knife is not into your throat yet. You can still speak. Now, who else gave the order to kill Bobby?"

The Cardinal gasped, trying to catch his breath. "It was Monsignor Tuppo."

"Who is he?"

"You saw him concelebrate Father Urrutia's mass with me." The Cardinal took a deep shuddering breath. "Now I have told you the truth. Will you let me go?"

"Who else is next on your list to kill?"

"No one, I swear."

"Lola Constantino, Father Bobby's assistant?"

"I..." The Cardinal gasped in pain. "We..."

"You're lying," Burt cut him.

"Alright, I admit..."

"Yes?"

"There are more..."

"Who else?"

"That, that woman."

"Lola? She's on your list?"

"Yes, yes."

"Who else? Father Tom Wheeler?"

"I don't know, I guess, yes, yes." The Cardinal rasped as he snaked his hand into a side table drawer and found the knife he kept nearby. "Now tell me, I have to know, one last thing. Do you have the *Yuz Asaf* document?"

"Something even better. I might have Jesus's bones."

"You lie, *Satana il Diavolo!*" "He stabbed the blade into Burt's arm.

Burt punched the Cardinal hard in the temple, stunning him. He took the knife away and threw it clattering across the marble floor. Dragging the prelate's unconscious body out of the bed he said, "Guess, you'll never have the chance to find out."

As the first morning light broke over Vatican City, the Sisters of Mercy who ran the Saint Bartholomew's Hospital on the *Isola Tibertina* island in the Tiber river, hurried across St. Peter's piazza. Saints of Christendom, including Moses and the twelve Apostles stared down at them from the twin arms that lovingly welcomed all the faithful into the square. Today was a special day because the nuns wanted to beat the crowds who would come to see Pope Leo lying in state inside the basilica.

The youngest nun, Sister Phillipa, actually only a postulant who had not yet taken her vows, was as usual in the lead as they scurried fast toward to the doors of St. Peter's and the chapel inside. Then, she slowed, staring up at the statue of St. Paul who had been given that special place next to St. Peter, directly above the Byzantine basilica's entrance. It took several seconds before the small group realized why Sister Phillipa was screaming. Looking up, they too saw the naked figure, neck and chest covered with black blood, hanging from a long rope. Tied to the feet of St. Paul, the Cardinal was dangling nearly over the front entrance to the basilica, obscenely swinging to and fro in the morning breeze, dripping gore onto the front steps.

The nuns crossed themselves. The mother superior ran to fetch the Swiss Guards at their station nearby. In the days ahead, there would be much speculation about who might have murdered such a high prelate, actually the most powerful Cardinal in the Curia. The killing of His Eminence, Cardinal Giuseppe Montalvo in such a gruesome manner, sent shock waves across the world.

One in particular, ex-General Obregon Saenz in Madrid, who was a member of the international governing board of the Hand of Christ, read about the atrocity and said to his wife, "I was against Montalvo's plot to kill Leo. I knew it. He went too far. Now we are paying the price. Get me Monsignor Tuppo on the line, please."

CHAPTER FORTY—ONE

After the ship *Bona Natalia* arrived in the port of Genoa, Lola took the train to Milan. At Malpensa airport, she boarded a flight without incident or interruption from authorities and flew to New York.

As the United Airlines plane flew close to New York city, the pilot said, "Ladies and gentlemen, we will be landing momentarily. For those seated on the left side of our craft, you can see the Statue of Liberty proudly holding her torch aloft. Welcome to America."

The green coated lady in the distance transfixed Lola. She seemed, as Burt said, somehow fitting.

Landing at JFK, Lola changed her plans. Instead of continuing onward to Kansas City on her ticket, she took an hour's ride in a taxi to the town of Beth Page which she researched on her iphone, was the home of the Italian Genealogical Group. That institution held a data base of all Italians who had come to New York and even the entire United States.

Arriving at the building housing the Genealogical Group, Lola requested a name she remembered well from long ago. Yes, the librarian checked, that person is living here. Yes, and here is an address. But I must first phone to see if he wishes to speak with you. It will be a charge of $5.00."

Lola paid her and the librarian scribbled a receipt. "Who shall I say is wishing to see him?

"Tell him Carla Contini is here." she said, knowing that she would be dead if that information got into the wrong hands.

The librarian called on her old style desk phone and asked for "Salvatore Abruzzo." When she had him on the phone, she detailed who was trying to reach him.

"An Italian relative you say?" the voice queried.

"I don't know that, sir. Her last name as I said, is Contini."

"Put her on," the man said.

She handed the phone to Lola who was standing nearby.

"*Ciao*," she said in greeting.

"Carla Contini?"

"Yes."

"Are you crazy coming here? You have a ten-million-dollar contract on your head."

"You are Vincenzo's brother," she said. "I was his wife. I did what I did for him."

"Don't talk to me any more on this phone."

"Will you see me?"

There was a long pause, then the voice said, "Where are you?"

"Beth Page."

"That is about thirty miles from here. It will take you about an hour. But not at my home. Do you know where Prospect Park is in Brooklyn?"

"Give me an address and I will find it."

"Meet me at the Boathouse in an hour. I won't wait any longer."

Lola took a taxi to Prospect Park. The driver got there in just over an hour but knew exactly where it was. In the sprawling five hundred and eighty-five-acre public park, the Boathouse was nestled in its Botanic Gardens.

There was no one there to meet her.

Lola sat on a bench that had a lovely view of the Brooklyn Bridge in the distance, watching locals with their children, riding the paddle boats, enjoying the sunny day, the lakes and flowers. She was holding the suitcase with the bones her lap, her traveling case near her when a man sat down beside her.

Turning, she had to catch her breath. She had forgotten how much Salvatore resembled his brother, her murdered husband, *Vincenzo*.

"You must be mad coming here," he glanced around warily.

"Do you think I would be here if it was not important?" she shot back.

"What do you want?"

"A favor."

"If anyone has recognized you," he said. "My family, everyone is *defunto*."

"You owe it to your brother, Vincenzo, to help me."

"I owe him nothing."

"With my *famiglia,* the Continis out of power and in prison, the Ruggieros have taken over that section of Napoli and rule there now."

"You put your family in prison. This is your doing, not mine."

"Naples is a long way from here."

'No, it is all around us, right here, as we speak."

"Don't quibble with me. I wish to have an audience with Don Ruggiero. I know he lives in Queens. The Italian Genealogical Group looked him up."

"Why?"

"Because he owes me. I put his family in charge."

Salvatore sighed. "Look," he said, "I know what you did. And I admire you for taking revenge for my brother. But that is all far away. I am a carpenter here now. I am an American. I have an honest life. I have nothing to do with the Ruggieros or any other *famiglia*. This is the past. And I wish to leave it there, inside the grave with Vincenzo." He crossed himself.

"Make the call and you are done," she said. "I will ask no more of you."

He thought about it. "I have a cousin who knows him."

"Have him make the call. I will pay him."

Salvatore stared at her. "There is no doubt you *are* a Contini. You have no fear, you are crazy, *pazzo*." This was said affectionately.

Standing, he pulled out his cell phone and walking away toward the pond, spoke to someone, gesticulating wildly with his hands. Finally, he closed the phone and came back to her.

"I don't know," he said. "My cousin, he does yard work for Don Ruggiero. This could just be a wild goose chase. Or worse you could be walking into a trap."

"I'll take my chances," Lola said. "Let's go."

"Go where?"

"Drive me there. Then you can leave."

"I never agreed to such a thing. And what is it in this suitcase you are carrying?" He pointed to the one beside her legs.

"My clothes."

"You always carry your clothes?"

"I came directly from the airport."

"And the other?"

"My lunch."

"Some big eater," he threw his hands up.

Salvatore picked up the suitcase on the ground and stomped across the lawn to a nearby parking lot. There he got into a battered Isuzu, its front right fender bent. Holding the case with the bones, Lola climbed inside.

It was not far. In about twenty minutes, they drove into an old neighborhood, filled with trees and parked in front of a small house. Salvatore called on his cell and a short, old man emerged from a side gate. He saw Salvatore and motioned toward the front door.

"That is *Icario*. You owe him a hundred bucks."

"And you?"

"I don't want any of your money." He spat out the window. "It is cursed."

When she got out, he drove away fast.

Lola went up the front walk and paid *Icario*. He said, "Knock on the screen door. She will let you in."

Lola mounted the steps of porch. The green-colored house was peeling and needed a paint job. In a moment, the door opened and an old woman said, "Yes?"

"I am Carla." Lola said.

"Come in, please." And when she was inside, said, "Follow me."

She led the way through the house, past statues of the Virgin and an ancient television set on a flimsy TV tray to the back door of his house, then outside, down wooden steps onto a tiny back yard lawn. "Don Ruggiero always likes to take his naps outside. He's done this for forty-five years. Can't stand being locked up inside a bedroom. Perhaps it was his time in prison that caused this. Who knows?"

At the back fence to the yard, the woman knocked on a gate and waited.

In a moment, a huge man in a pin-striped suit and tie opened it and she told him the visitor Don Ruggiero was expecting had arrived.

"He has already retired and is sleeping," the guard responded, shooting Lola a sour look. "You are too late."

"Don't talk that way," the woman scolded him in Italian. "Have some manners. Don't you know my husband has already approved this?"

"It is important," Lola told him. "A matter of *famiglia*."

"You? What would you know about *famiglia*?" the bodyguard spat. Then he looked at the old woman. "If it were up to me, she would not enter."

"You do not make decisions around here. You are told what to do."

"*Si*, I will do my duty."

"Then do it quickly," she ordered him.

He grunted something, then said, "Wait here."

He closed the gate.

The old woman said, "My husband sleeps out here under the stars. It does not matter the weather. He likes to breathe the fresh air."

"Even when it snows?" Lola asked.

"Ah, he has an electric blanket for the winter." She smiled. "And of course there is me."

The gate opened again and the bodyguard said, "What is in the suitcases you carry?"

"None of your business," Lola answered. "It is my luggage. I came from the airport to see Don Ruggiero."

"Let her inside," the woman said. "I will take responsibility."

The bodyguard shrugged, stepped aside, then motioned Lola to enter. "Don Ruggiero is still awake. You are lucky."

She entered a fragrant garden, filled with lilacs and roses and a sweeping lawn that fed down to an enormous canopy of parachute silk, shading an old man who lay propped up by pillows, on a king size bed. He looked curiously at Lola as she approached.

Lola stopped at the foot of his bed and said to him, "Don Ruggiero, I am sorry to disturb your rest."

The Don, who appeared to be in his 80s with short-cropped white hair, waved the apology away with a flick of his hand. "*Da dove viene?*" he inquired. "*Napoli?*"

"*Niente,*" Lola replied. "Roma. I live in hiding. I am another person now."

He nodded, understanding. The bodyguard who was standing nearby, grunted noisily.

"*Disturbo?*" she asked the enormous man.

"Remo does not approve of you," the Don explained, "and for that matter neither do I." He patted the bed. Tentatively, Lola sat on the edge.

"In Naples," she said, "I took my revenge for my husband, Vincenzo. And my family lost everything to you."

"A terrible thing you did," he said. "You are considered a whore, a *traditore.*"

"But you profited, did you not?"

The Don stared emotionless with rheumy eyes.

"And with what I have done, with the gift I have given you, I come, seeking a simple gift in return."

"You gave me nothing," he said finally. "I took it."

"Yes," she agreed. "But I made it possible."

The old man shrugged, not giving any clue as to what he was thinking. "What do you want?"

Lola leaned close, whispering her request.

When she was done, Don Ruggiero asked, "What you want hidden is inside your case?"

"Yes."

"Is it money? Something of great value?"

"Yes and no. Not money or gold or anything like that. It is personal. Tell me, can you do what I request?"

"It is most unusual demand. But it is possible." The Don studied her momentarily.

"Can I trust you?"

At that, the Don looked offended. "You of all people dare ask me that?"

"*Scuzi*. But it might occur to you or that big slab of beef standing behind me to turn me in for a big reward. I have heard my head is worth ten million dollars. "

"And how would I collect that?" Ruggiero wondered. "From my enemies? Don't be *stupido*. They would never pay up. However, to do this, I will need a little *pizzo*. How much did the Italian government pay you for snitching?"

She had anticipated his greed. "When I received my new identity, I took away a reward that I have not touched. Two million dollars are in a Swiss account."

"That amount is correct," Ruggiero's dim eyes lit up. "What you wish me to do will cost two million."

"I will pay you five hundred thousand dollars and no more," she said.

"One million." The Don rubbed his shrunken, heavily veined hands together. "And that is my final offer."

"I must have proof and personally see that it is done."

"You shall."

"Then it is a deal?"

Hearing that, Don Ruggiero reached out, took her hand, and kissed it. Then he lay back on his gigantic bed, and pulling the silk quilt to his chin, closed his eyes.

"*Sono contento,*" he said.

CHAPTER FORTY—TWO

Danny Sirizo worked for the National Parks Service and was assigned a great deal of his time to maintaining the sidewalks, railings and bathrooms on Ellis Island. Lately, he had been promoted to repairing various parts of the Statue of Liberty. His particular area of responsibility was the gigantic platform on which the "Lady with the Light" stood. The top pedestal was made of granite brought from Leete's Island, Connecticut, and its understructure was heavily reinforced concrete. What with the high winds, freezing rain and salt from the ocean around it, the statue's huge foundation was always in need of repair.

"Tomorrow," Danny joked to Lola, "I must plug beneath the lady's toes. Drill out some rotten stone masonry and put in epoxy. Her feet, made of copper, are as big as this house."

His wife, Amelia added proudly, "Did you know her official title is Liberty Enlightening the World? There are broken chains lying beside her feet."

Lola had listened to Danny and liked the way he felt such pride in dealing with the Statue.

"I need six ladders even to reach beneath her toes. All together she is three hundred and five feet tall."

"And no one can see you once you are up there on the base?"

"No tourist, no guards, nobody. I am totally out of sight. It is very cold, windy and dangerous there. No one ever comes up there but me."

"I have heard there is a viewing room in her crown."

"*Sí*, but they cannot look down at her toes. And you cannot see her feet from the ocean either. They are too high. But there is a problem. Since 9/11, there is much security. They check everything. Even my tools and the special plastic cement I use."

"Then how will you get my package up there?"

"Once I am out of sight, I will pull it up by rope."

"How do you get the rope up there?"

"I will accidentally leave it the night before and lower one end where no one can see."

She nodded and opened the Samsonite case. Inside were twenty-two objects wrapped in clinging transparent plastic film, then placed in heavy duty hermetically sealed plastic bags.

"Ah, whatever you have is shrink wrapped and in a vacuum. Very good. The weather will never affect your package."

"And if they are additionally placed inside your repair, they should be safe."

"*Certo*, do you want the entire case placed in the repair?"

"Is it big enough?"

"I could put my kitchen in her toe," he laughed.

Lola placed a heavy padlock on the suitcase's handle, and snapped it shut. "Then *in bocca al lupo*," she said. Good luck. Or literally, "Go into the wolf's mouth."

"*Crepi il lupo!*" he answered correctly. "And may the wolf croak."

CHAPTER FORTY—THREE

It had been raining in downpours across Italy for the past few days. Schools were shut in some cities and a small bridge collapsed in the southern province of Calabria, killing a man. More than one hundred puppies perished after a kennel flooded. Forty-some Boy Scouts were rescued from Mount Etna in Sicily after becoming stranded in the unusual deluge nationwide. The intense storms were also accompanied by severe wind gusts of up to 70 mph. Rain fell between 2-4 inches per hour.

In Rome, the inhabitants braced for the deluge. The last time the city flooded was in 1876. Now that the Tiber river basin had been widened and covered in concrete, there had been no more devastating flooding or landslides. Still, with most of Rome lying in flatlands, the worse storms, like the one that occurred in 2008, could alarmingly raise the river water within a few feet of its many bridges. Now this severe storm was flooding sewers, disrupting train and bus services, so Rome's mayor had declared a state of emergency. In addition, the *Aniene* river running through the city's northeast burst its banks, forcing police to seal off nearby areas and block off a major road leading into Rome.

In this mess, Burt had moved several times, making sure he remained elusive. Now, he was residing at a pilgrim's hotel called *Gesu Infante,* on the *Via dei Coronari* which overlooked the *Castel' San Angelo* bridge that spanned the swollen and rising Tiber. From his window, he watched as the yellowish torrent edged up higher. He had chosen this hotel partly because German faithful stayed there and the police would not think of looking for him there. But more importantly because it gave him a great view of the *Castel San Angelo* bridge below.

Workers who lived inside Vatican City used either the *Ponte Vittorio Emanuelle II* bridge or the *Castel' San Angelo* to cross over the Tiber and return to their homes or shop in Rome. He had kept a careful watch on both bridges. Last

Friday, Monsignor Anselmo Tuppo, his next and final target, had crossed the Tiber on the San Angelo. Now it was Friday again and he waited.

During these last days, he had not heard from Lola. He expected that since he told her not to break her silence unless necessary for fear of alerting the Hand of Christ to her location. He kept the prospect of meeting her again bright in his mind once he was finished here. In order to stay in touch and be able to contact her and Inspector Jodpat, the Interpol cop in Delhi, for any news about Bobby or the autopsy on Kali, Burt bought a Vodafone 228 black, cell phone. The storekeeper told him he must show his passport and buy a SIM card for it to work. Burt was careful to pay cash, about 25 Euros, but did not like the fact he had used his passport. Still it was either that or be unable to communicate.

He rang Inspector Jodpat several times, hoping to hear any news. But each time he was out of the office. And though he was tempted, he did not contact Lola.

He watched the TV for any news about Montalvo's murder and saw Italian police and the lab people in white suits at the crime scene inside Montalvo's bedroom and later in front of St. Peter's basilica. Because he had worn gloves, he knew they would find no fingerprints on the body or anywhere. Bobby's priest suit and shoes he had burned in a city garbage incinerator. And as for the climbing rope, Burt had paid for that with cash at an RAI sporting goods store, making it untraceable. The broken cross he had thrown in the Tiber. The only item he had kept was the Cardinal's .25 caliber derringer.

That evening, after returning to his room from a dinner of pasta and olive oil, Burt's cell phone vibrated inside his pocket. He saw it was Lola calling. He knew this must be something very important for her to violate their agreement. Opening the cell, he immediately saw an image of the Statue of Liberty bobbing unsteadily on the horizon. It looked like it was being shot from a boat.

"I took this on my cellphone on my way over this morning on the ferry," a man's voice announced. "Now I am playing it back for you so you can see everything.""He's doing it," Lola whispered to Burt.

He recognized her voice. "Doing what?"

"Putting the package on the place I chose. The Statue of Liberty. A fitting place, no?"

Burt grinned. It was brilliant. "It's got meaning alright," he said.

As he watched, the man with the phone camera, partially revealed in tan overalls, the wind whipping his clothes, climbed up a thin metal ladder. A section of one of the Statue of Liberty's enormous green feet came into view. As the worker stepped onto the base of the statue, he could see a giant stone chain she had shattered. Standing next to it, the worker was dwarfed.

"Who is he?"

"With the National Park Service. I hired him.""Can he hear us?" Burt asked.

"No, the playback is just one way. We hear him, no more."

Now, Burt could clearly make out the worker leaning over the edge of a large pedestal and pull up a rope.

"See the inscription on her foot?" Lola asked.

Burt looked. "I see it. It says 'Freedom from Oppression and Tyranny'."

"Good, huh?"

"Nice going." He knew what had attracted Lola to put the bones there.

"As I said, no tourist, nobody can see up here," the man now continued in his wind-slapped narration. He bent over, looking down at the water below, pointing the phone's camera toward the statue's base far below to reveal the morning's boatloads of tourists scurrying along a pier. Then he tilted up to the horizon and they could see he was high above New York Harbor on the pedestal.

"My job is never done," the man explained. "Just look at how her robe is being eaten up by the salt air and rust."

Tilting the camera straight up, the statue's moss-colored, copper gown come into the picture. It was riddled with quarter-size holes, eaten through by corrosion.

"Guy's a film director," Burt commented.

Swinging the camera around to show himself in a Selfie, he smiled and said, "It is I, Danny, National Park Service repairman at your service."

"He's from a family of show-offs." Lola whispered. "I remember in *Napoli*, his uncle would dance like a bear for people on street corners for money."

Now, Danny carefully set the camera down, propping it exactly so the frame revealed the big toe. It was the size of a Volkswagen. "You see how gigantic she is?" He tenderly stroked the statue's foot and then the ankle. "A big woman, no? And so beautiful."

They watched as he bent and untied the rope from the Samsonite suitcase's handle. He lifted it into frame.

"See? Closed tight. Just like you locked it."

Wind gusting against him, Danny adjusted the camera's view to a precisely-cut, four-inch wide, three feet deep excavation in the base beneath her toe.

"Here is the repair I started yesterday. The cement inside the marble was crumbling and I have taken out all the rotten pieces. Now I will repair it by inserting your package and fill it over with a waterproof cement that comes special from Iran. It is the best cement in the world. Very, very strong."

Danny carefully placed the Samsonite into the hole. It fit perfectly.

"How sad," Lola remarked. "That we have to do this."

"Whatever happens it will be here someday."

The workman expertly mixed water from his tool box with a canvas bag of cement, and began to trowel it in the repair, sealing it.

"Have we become like the Hand of Christ? Willing to do anything?" Lola wondered.

I always was, Burt was tempted to respond, but said nothing.

When the repair was finished, Danny looked into the camera, "Are you satisfied? I did my best. I have fulfilled my end of the bargain."

Lola, unable to answer, said nothing.

"*Ciao.*" He snapped shut the cell phone, ending the transmission.

"Did you see it all?" she asked Burt when the little screen went blank.

"Great job."

"And you are done too?"

"Almost. I'll call you tomorrow after I'm finished."

"I'll be waiting, my love," she said.

CHAPTER FORTY—FOUR

Last Friday had been a holy terror of a day for Monsignor Tuppo. Against every piece of his common sense, he had ventured forth from his safe retreat inside Vatican City where he had been ordered to stay and had gone to visit his boys in Civitavecchia. Returning finally in the early morning hours, he had been shaking so badly at what he had done that he found he had to drink nearly an entire bottle of altar wine. How had he been so stupid? Wasn't it enough that Cardinal Montalvo had only recently perished at the hands of a murderer? Why had he exposed himself to such great danger? The answer was simple. When it came to having sex with children, Tuppo had no control over himself. He was worse than an alcoholic. A drug addict on crack. A man with a terrible, destructive habit. He was a sex maniac, a hebephiliac, simply out of control. Primarily attracted to boys who have at least started puberty and have signs of adult sexual maturation, his vice was preteens between 11 and 14 years old—all migrants in one house from Syria and Africa.

Now as his usual day of visit on a Friday approached once again, Tuppo dreaded at what he was leaning toward doing. What he had been consistently doing for years. He made himself a promise to be strong. He would not go out. He would handle it. He could overcome his urges this time.

Then the call came.

The new head of the Hand of Christ, retired General Obregon Saenz, in his office in Madrid rang him and after the customary pleasantries, said, "*Monsignore, we* know about your little habit."

"I don't know what you are talking about," Tuppo protested.

"We all have our little failings," the General said. "I am not calling to scold you. Instead, what I want you to do this Friday is go, as usual, to your place of pleasure."

Tuppo, sitting in his librarian's office in the Vatican Archives, looked out the window and saw black skies above and solid sheets of rain whipping across St. Peter's piazza below. "I do not think that is a good idea, General. There is a terrible storm here. The Tiber is up near its banks. Some streets are flooded."

"Alright, you don't have to go all the way to Civitavecchia. We need you just to go as far as the bridge."

"What bridge?"

"The one you always take. Don't play games with me, Tuppo."

"But it is too dangerous. The river even now I can see is splashing across the *Altoviti* road that runs on the other side of it."

"Listen carefully to what I have to say," the General enunciated the words with great deliberation. "My conversation with you must necessarily be vague. We do not know who is listening. This phone is not secure."

"I understand. I am listening."

"There is someone you know. Someone Cardinal Montalvo, God rest his soul, *used* in the past."

Tuppo know he was speaking of Massimo. He felt himself shudder at the name.

"Now he has informed me that his very sophisticated unit in Switzerland has, through several satellites they lease time on, triangulated a cell phone call that was made near the bridge."

"Who are we speaking of?"

"No names," the general cut him off. "All you need to know, for your part, is that, at your usual time, you must walk across the bridge. The rest will be taken care of."

"General," the Monsignor pleaded, his voice shaking. "I don't want any part of this. Don't you know what happened to Cardinal Montalvo?"

"This is a direct order, Monsignor," the General barked. "After this, and only after this, is your part in the disastrous affair with Pope Leo expunged. If you do not obey, there will be serious consequences." And General Obregon Saenz hung up.

Tuppo stared for a long time at the ancient San Angelo bridge he could see below. The bridge of ten angels, five on each side, that directly connected the Vatican to Rome. The bridge he loved so much, lined by Seraphim depicting the passion of Christ, holding a throne, whips, the crown of thorns, Veronica's Veil,

Jesus' garment and dice, the nails used to crucify him, the cross, the Sponge, the Lance and his favorite, the Superscription, a list of those going to heaven.

After a while, he realized he was still holding the phone in his hand. It took Tuppo several tries before he was able to put the receiver back into its cradle.

***

He chose the Russian-made Dragunov. It was a decent sniper rifle with an effective range of only 800 meters which made it limiting. But the Dragunov's barrel was fitted with a slotted flash suppressor which hid the shooter's position. The bullets it fired were 7.62x54mm, small for a kill. So the shot had to be extremely accurate. But thankfully, Massimo had been able to obtain ten specialized sniper cartridges, developed by Sabelnikov and Dvorianinov, that had a steel core for maximum terminal effect.

Normally, he would have considered this gambit a long shot. How could they be certain that the priest's brother was actually here? Still he had relied on the nerds in Switzerland before and this time they were confident of his presence somewhere near the *Castel San Angelo* bridge. Previously, they had identified Lola Constantino's cell phone number, used first as early as the Rome train station in which his beloved sister had staged her assassination of the priest from Turin. Now a call from her had come from New York and been traced to an end point *somewhere* near the bridge. The registered owner of that phone, it turned out, was the American cop, Burt Powell who had purchased it several days before. Massimo guessed that the cop had been very busy recently, killing Cardinal Montalvo. And it stood to reason that his next victim might be Monsignor Angelo Tuppo. It was a long shot, but all he had.

General Obregon Saenz in Madrid had ordered Massimo to take a position high up behind one of the cylindrical-shaped Castle's crenellations and wait. That the museum would be closed to the public that day. He told Massimo that Tuppo had developed the habit of crossing that bridge every Friday so it seemed a good hunch that Powell knew it and was waiting for him.

Still, doubts nagged him. Perhaps Tuppo would today choose to cross over the other bridge nearby, the *Vittorio Emanuelle*. At any rate, Massimo thought it was only for one day. He would play the cards dealt him and hope for the best. Gaining his position on the top of The Castle of The Holy Angel who was blowing his golden trumpet above him, Massimo began his watch on the bridge below.

***

At just before six p.m., in the dying light, from his hotel window in his room inside the *Gesu Infante*, amid the tourists with umbrellas turned inside out by the lashing wind and the workers heading home from the Vatican, Burt saw the unmistakable figure of Monsignor Anselmo Tuppo begin to cross the bridge below. He was wearing civilian clothes but there was no doubt with his bald head, skinny shoulders hunched forward and his lurching steps against the wind gusts, that it was the Monsignor. The river below had swollen higher and was running extremely fast now. It would be a simple thing to make it look like an accident and bump him over the railing into the raging waters, letting him drown. Once that was done, he reasoned, Father Wheeler and all Lola's and Bobby's friends would be safer. And his work here would be finished. Quickly pulling on a blue anorak and lifting the hood over his face, Burt scrambled down the hotel stairs and splashed across the street onto the bridge.

Situated behind the very top wall, on what was originally Hadrian's mausoleum, and which was now a museum, Massimo swept the scope of the Dragunov across the bridge. He hated this high wind. It was always a sniper's worse enemy. In the blasts, his site was jumping back and forth. Something he reminded himself he must correct for on the shot.

He had arrived early and spent the day watching the bridge, eating his lunch of salami, cheese and bread. All day, there was no sign of Tuppo or the American cop. Toward evening, as he polished off his third bottle of water, and was about to give up, he saw Tuppo appear at the bridge's edge below and hesitate. Quickly, he focused the scope, searching, hoping to see the priest's brother appear.

Tuppo began running now, splashing in the rain, across the long bridge, heading to what Massimo thought was the taxi stand on the other side. He checked again. Still there was no sign of the brother. Silently, Massimo cursed. It had all been for nothing. Then as Tuppo gained the halfway point on the bridge, a square-shouldered man ran toward him. It was Powell. Carefully, Massimo checked the scope's information read out. The distance was six hundred and twenty-seven yards. He sighted on the torso of Burt Powell. A head shot was too iffy in this wind and downpour.

In the driving rain, Monsignor Tuppo sprinted across the bridge. His heart was beating so hard it felt like it wanted out of his chest. His breathing was ragged and he had only one goal: to make it across this cursed bridge and on the other side escape in a taxi to Civitavecchia. It took him a moment to realize who was coming directly at him.

***

From his perch, Massimo sighted on Burt and was squeezing the trigger, when he saw to his surprise, that he had grabbed hold of Tuppo. He had his arms wrapped around him and was standing directly in front of him. His head hidden, he did not present a clear shot.

Face running with rivulets of rain, Burt said, "Hello, Monsignor Anselmo Tuppo."

"I never, I never." Tuppo tried to wriggle away and escape.

"Yes, you did," he said. "It was as much you as Montalvo who killed Bobby. How does it feel to pay the price?"

Burt lifted him off his feet and carried him to the railing.

"What are you doing?" Tuppo cried.

Making a split second decision, Massimo pulled the trigger. There was very little recoil because the escaping gas of the bullet cushioned it.

The bullet struck Monsignor Tuppo in the back of the head, spiraled through his skull as Massimo had concluded it would, came out his eye and would have killed Burt too. But in the wind, the slug, deflected slightly at this distance, whipped instead past his ear.

Still holding Tuppo's corpse, Burt realized what was happening. Before he could locate Massimo, there was another blast that buried itself in Tuppo's back. This time the projectile pierced through the spine and lung and roared out of his chest, striking Burt so hard in his shoulder that it flung him away from the Monsignor's lifeless body.

Fighting a wave of unconsciousness, Burt crawled through the puddled water on the bridge toward the safety of a parapet.

His direct sightline obstructed, Massimo fired twice anyway. The first slug hit the angel holding the thorns, chinking a piece of plaster off his halo. The second tore a hole through the angel's robe.

Quickly sighting once again, he saw that the priest's brother had pulled himself behind the railing and was partially hidden. People who were crossing the bridge, and seeing Tuppo fall, now panicked and began to run. Cursing, Massimo ran down the steps of the Castle to finish the job.

***

Burt had been shot but was alive. His left side ached as he looked up, searching for the shooter. In the rush of bodies flashing past him, he spotted Massimo coming down the outside steps of the Castle, sniper rifle in hand. Momentarily, he thought about releasing his hold on this balustrade and off he would sail down the river, taking his chances in the flood waters. But in the swollen gray roaring mass, he saw logs and rubbish, roofs of buildings floating by. A bad choice. He looked again and saw Massimo now on the bridge, rifle to his shoulder, sighting on him. Realizing his lack of options, Burt slid through the open marble railing and fell toward the torrent.

Seeing that, Massimo fired. In the squall, he couldn't tell if he hit him. Massimo ignored the people screaming and running and hurried to the bridge's marble railing. Leaning over, he searched the fast flowing river water.

"Hello, asshole," a voice said from below.

Massimo looked down. What he saw was the priest's brother holding himself by one hand, his feet dragging behind him in the tumbling water. In his free hand, he held a small derringer.

"Compliments of your boss, Cardinal Montalvo." Burt pulled the trigger. The small .25 caliber slug made a perfect, pencil-sized hole in Massimo's forehead. The assassin fell forward, his Dragunov flying, body draped limply over the railing.

Burt started to struggle up. But to his surprise, he saw a tumbling car scrape the underside of the bridge and barrel toward him. Pulling him under, it swept him away.

CHAPTER FORTY—FIVE

Ebbetsburg, Kansas

Lola arrived from New York at the Denver international airport and rented a car which she drove for six hours across the flat plains of Colorado, then across the state line into Ebbetsburg, Kansas, population 8,243. She drove past Wally's Furniture store, the IPA grocery store, St. Sebastian's Catholic church and ironically St. Paul's Presbyterian next to the police station. The streets were lined with tall cottonwood, their green leaves blowing in the constant wind that never seemed to let up.

Finding the address Burt had given her months ago, Lola alighted from the rented Chevrolet and stood before his simple, single story, white clapboard house. She knocked on the door and when no one answered, crossed the front yard. It had been a long journey. And somehow, even as she had left JFK, she hoped that Burt would be there to greet her. Now she realized that wish had been in vain.

Circling behind the house to the propane tank, she fumbled beneath its cap lid, and found the key Burt said would be there. But as she turned toward his back door, a voice said, "Hold it right there."

Lola spun to see a buff woman in police uniform. "Can I ask what you're doing here?"

"I am Lola Constantino, a friend of Burt Powell," she held up the key. "He is letting me stay here."

"Burt never said anything to me," the woman said. "Been gone a long time too. Where you from anyway, with that accent?"

"Italy," Lola said.

"Yeah, I guess that figures. It's where he went. Anyway." She looked her up and down.

"Are you Angie?" Lola asked. "Burt told me about you."

"He told you about me?" the officer, looked concerned.

"All good things," Lola assured her.

"Well," Angie shrugged, "I guess he would at that."

Lola felt the Kansas breeze lift the trees around the house. "Did Father Bobby's casket arrive?"

"Came yesterday, as a matter of fact. The pastor is waiting on hearing all the facts. Said he needs to know where to bury him. I told him to just cool his heels until we get it all sorted out."

"Sorted out?"

"You know, if Father Bobby, you know, did himself."

"He was murdered," Lola said. "We are waiting proof of that from an Interpol officer."

"Somebody foreign did call the station earlier this week. An Officer Jodpat, or someone like that, I think. I wrote it down. Said he wanted to talk to Burt."

"Then perhaps there is news." Lola brightened enthusiastically. "Is there any word from Burt?"

"None that I heard. Where is he?"

"In Rome," Lola said. "He'll be here when he's finished."

"Finished doing what?"

"Just wrapping up some loose ends." Lola said. "He has a cell and I tried to call him. But there was no connection."

"Must have been something important for Burt to have a cell phone. He hated those things." She started toward the back door. "We'll call that fellow Jodpat tomorrow from my office," Angie said. "In the meantime, let's get you inside. Check on the food supply. Burt kept the place pretty well stocked. I mean there's probably beans anyway. You know how men are, enough to eat and get by on. We should see if there are any critters in the bedroom. I expect that is where you will sleep."

"I hadn't thought about it," Lola said.

"Well," Angie said, opening the door, "by the looks of you, I'd say it's where you'll wind up."

"This is, how do you say, awkward," Lola said, stepping inside.

"Awkward ain't the half of it," Angie replied.

The next morning, as a result of Lola's call to Inspector Rohan Jodpat in India, he detailed the findings in the autopsy of Kali Mohi in which a state pathologist had found a spent slug lodged in his backbone. In turn, that bullet had matched the Glock that Delicata Fabrizio had used as the murder weapon.

In a strange twist, a beggar from inside the temple had come forward, declaring he was a witness to Bobby's murder. He had sought to claim the reward of !000 rupees, about $14.90, a standard sum offered by the Indian government to anyone who was willing to testify in a capital case. At the time, he had been ignored by police because he was a low caste. Muzzafaro, reviewing the files, had discovered the man's testimony. Oh, the beggar also claimed that he saw this killer, dressed like some outrageous Japanese cartoon character, take Father Bobby's body to a bridge and hang it there."

Lola gasped and covered her mouth in astonishment at hearing this break-through.

"Congratulations to you and Burt," Inspector Rohan chimed in his Indian accent to Lola. "Your efforts proved out."

"Many thanks to you, Inspector. I know how hard you worked to get all this done."

"You are most welcome. It is nothing more than doing our duty, I assure you. I, too, am most pleased that justice has been done. There is one matter, however. I have received a complaint from the district of Kashmir, the city of Srinagar, to be exact. It seems someone violated a tomb and made off with some holy bones. Do you possibly know anything about that?"

"You took us out in your own helicopter," she said. "Did you see us carrying anything?"

There was a pause, then Inspector Jodpat said, "I must tell you, I have learned from my superior in the capitol, that the Indian Prime Minister, learning of the theft of the bones, wants no part of their return or presence. He feels that the bones would bring nothing but more trouble between Hindi and Muslims. Do you understand?"

After a few more pleasantries, and a promise to send an official copy of the reports, Rohan signed off.

Angie, who had been listening on the other line, said, "What's with the bones?"

"Just some relics Father Bobby found," Lola said.

"Do you have them?"

"Thank God, no," Lola said. Thanking her for the use of the phone, she started out of the office.

"Lola," Angie said, "I know what Burt is like. I'm not saying anything about him. But he had certain ways. Even before he left, there was some talk about an investigation into the disappearance of a criminal. And to tell you the truth, there had been other pieces of shit who just vanished. I agree that every one of them was bad and deserved what he got. But that doesn't make it right, you get my drift? I can't stand around as an officer of the law and abide such a thing. And while I am hoping Burt is alright and alive, I also hope he does not come back here. It would just complicate things."

***

The next day, Lola called *Ispectore* Zighette in Rome and told him Burt wanted to bury his brother Bobby in Kansas. The officer said Burt had mentioned that and he would comply with his wishes and ship the body. Lola offered to the pay the costs.

Changing subjects, Zighette asked if she knew where Burt was?

"Why? The question made her shudder.

"I recently received an intriguing report. Several witnesses say they saw a man shot on the *Castel San Angelo* bridge. That body it turned out belonged to a Monsignor Anselmo Tuppo."

Lola held her breath and listened as the officer continued.

"The assassin in turn was killed. And a third man swept away in the flooded river."

"How strange," Lola managed. "do you have any idea who it was?"

"One of the passersby took some photos of the incident. But was raining and we are studying the rather fuzzy pictures now. Eight bodies have been found floating in the Tiber. Two more washed all the way out to sea at Ostia. None have yet been identified. But I will be in touch as I get to the bottom of this mystery. Give *Tenente* Powell, my regards."

When Lola disconnected, she wondered if Zighette knew more than he was telling her. Was he telling her Burt was part of that scene on the *Castel San Angelo* bridge? Had he fallen in the flood water? If so, had he survived? A million bad thoughts would keep her awake during the following nights as she worried.

The beggar witness's report on seeing Father Bobby murdered arrived by FAX from Inspector Jodpat. The local Bishop in Denver, Colorado acceded to its findings and Father Bobby was allowed to be buried in hallowed soil, inside the church's cemetery. His head would be pointing toward the altar in the manner and honor given to all good priests.

However, even after Bobby's body arrived, Lola held off on the funeral, hoping Burt would show up. But after a week when he did not, she arranged for the ceremony.

In St. Sebastian's church cemetery that overlooked wheat and barley fields below, a small congregation surrounded Father Bobby's casket as final prayers and blessings were pronounced over him by the pastor. Aunts, uncles, nephews and nieces arrived from all over the Midwest. At the end of the ceremony, after each spoke praises and shared good memories of Bobby, the crowd headed toward the church's basement for the customary meal to be served by the Ladies Altar Society.

Lola, who had not spoken, held back, waiting until the parish priest, relatives and friends bid their farewells at Father Bobby's coffin. Alone now, as the Kansas breeze picked up and blew against her, rocking the coffin a little on its gurney above the grave, she allowed her mind to roam over all that had happened from the first time she had met Bobby to winding up on the long trek with Burt in India. What a quest, she thought. It occurred to her that through all this, the *Yuz Asaf,* the ancient document Bobby had taken from the Vatican archives and that had caused all this trouble had never been found.

She grinned, rising, "And only you know where you put it. *Arrivederci,* my wonderful friend. Until we see each other again."

Bending, she kissed the casket, then walked away as the cemetery workers who had stood off and waited reverently, now moved in with a skip loader to lower the casket into the ground and cover it with fresh earth.

CHAPTER FORTY—SIX

Rome, Italy

Another month passed before *Ispectore* Zighette sent e-mails detailing the identities of several bodies recovered from the flooding of the Tiber. None were Burt. The tall man with a small bullet hole in his forehead appeared to be, by his faint fingerprints, Massimo Fabrizio, a well-known assassin. He had suffered powder burns and been shot at close range. There was no trace of the third man who had killed him.

On top of Leo XIV being assassinated by a car bomb, and Cardinal Giuseppe Montalvo hung from the feet of the statue of St. Paul in St. Peter's square, and now the head librarian of the Vatican Archives murdered, Vatican City locked itself down in an atmosphere of fear and unapproachability.

The four gates in the wall, including the Vatican Railway Station, admitted few and those only after thorough searches. Commerce slowed to a crawl. Tourists admitted into St. Peter's basilica and the Sistine chapel with its marvelous murals painted by Michelangelo, were forced to go through detectors and full body scans. For a while, the Vatican museums were shuttered and turned away tourists. But realizing how much money the museums brought in, Vatican hierarchy posted additional guards and they were re-opened.

Cardinal Reynaldo Storche, newly elected, ordered the Hand of Christ's organization to relocate from within the Vatican walls to Madrid, Spain. With the death of its powerful leader, Cardinal Montalvo, the group had no recourse but to leave and set up operations there. Under General Saenz the Hand quickly reorganized, receiving massive infusions of money from worldwide wealthy donors.

CHAPTER FORTY—SEVEN

During long, restless nights, she tossed in Burt's bed. Then toward morning, after finally falling asleep, she would see Burt drowned and startle up, her face wet with tears.

Over time, the sinking feeling that Burt was in her past, permanently gone, began to seep into her as truth. She fought it but knew if he was alive, he would have somehow contacted her by now. Even if he was badly hurt. Every week she visited Father Bobby's grave only to see the date on his tombstone and each time feel that somehow that he was giving her a message. She must start her life over.

Awaking at sunrise, she packed her few things inside her carry-on and saw the weather had turned nasty. The skies were black with towering thunderheads and roiling with heavy clouds traveling fast overhead. She had returned the rented Chevy to Hertz months ago, so she walked down to the Greyhound bus station Passing the police station, she thought about stopping and saying goodbye to Angie. But she knew there was no affection between them and she did not feel like pretending.

Inside the bus station, the woman, whom she knew from St, Sebastian's altar society, greeted her.

"I need to buy a ticket," Lola told her.

"To where?"

"I don't know." She hesitated.

The woman reached across the counter and touched her hand. "Are you sure?" she asked.

"He is not coming," Lola said, fighting back tears. "I have to move on."

The woman asked sympathetically, "Why not wait a little longer? Give it a few more days. Miracles do happen, you know."

Lola shook her head. She had no faith that Burt had survived the terrible flood in Rome. She knew for sure that if he was alive, he would have moved heaven and hell to let her know he was okay.

"Tell you what, let's pray together," the woman said. "Just give it a minute. What's a minute, huh?"

Lola, more to humor her than anything, nodded and together the two closed their eyes.

The door opened behind them and a man entered. He was a postman and had the walking route in town. When he saw the two women silent in prayer, he waited respectfully and when they had finished, approached the ticket counter.

"Herbie," the Greyhound woman said. "Good morning."

"Morning," he said, "I hope I'm not disturbing anything."

"Oh, no, we were just saying a prayer for guidance."

"Well, I hope you get it." He cleared his throat. "I need to buy a ticket for my niece. She's coming down from Tulsa to visit us. I'd like to send it to her."

Lola said she would wait and sat down on the bench.

When the transaction was completed, Herbie bid the Greyhound lady goodbye, then started out. "Oh," he said, "you're Lola Constantino, right?"

Lola nodded.

"There's a little package came this morning for you. Save me time if I could just hand it to you here."

"Who's it from?"

"No return address or name of sender. Hold on. I'll get it. I was going to deliver it to you later today at Burt's place. But I guess it's okay you have it now."

The woman behind the counter and Lola locked eyes.

With the Post Office just next door, Herbie returned in a flash, holding a small, brown paper-wrapped package about the size of a rifle bullet.

"This is for me?" Lola wondered.

"Got your name on it in tiny print. Address too."

Momentarily, Lola took it and turned it in her hands, examining it.

"Aren't you gonna open it?" the woman behind the counter wondered.

Lola tore off the wrapping.

"What the hey?" the woman asked. "Is this some kind of joke?"

"No, no," Lola blurted, tears flooding her eyes, "It's exactly what I wanted!"

"You know, I never seen one looks quite like that," Herbie studied it. "Fact is, this one looks different somehow. And look there where it's made."

Turning the pack of Juicy Fruit over, Lola saw that the gum was manufactured at 1035 McTavisa Road, Calgary, Canada.

"Well, I knew it. Look at that," Herbie announced. "I knew it didn't look right. Has a different color. Not exactly yellow like it should be."

Lola clutched the gum hard in her hand. She turned to the woman. "I know where I'm going now."

"Do you?" she asked, astonished.

"I know exactly where."

"Praise God! He does work in mysterious ways," the Greyhound woman said.

EPILOGUE

Haya Maloof had arrived in Rome a few months ago, a Christian immigrant fleeing the carnage of Syria. She had left behind her husband and three children and hoped to make enough money to someday bring them over and live with her. It had been her good fortune to approach the North American college and gain employment as a janitor and room maid.

Haya was working through the college professors' wing, cleaning their rooms as usual. She had been notified that a new resident would be moving into the room she was cleaning now. When she began on the bathroom, she found there was something wrong with the toilet. For some reason, it would not flush properly. The tank would keep filling unless she jiggled the handle.

Removing the lid, she saw that at the bottom of the tank, someone had placed a river stone about the size of a brick. She knew this was an old trick to save water. But then Haya saw there was something pinned underneath the rock. She reached down into the tank and pulled out the stone, revealing a plastic, sealed baggy that had been held beneath it. Nervously, she checked around to see if anyone was watching her, then lifted the dripping bag out and opened it. Inside was a perfectly dry ancient-looking piece of parchment, rolled into a scroll and held together by a red ribbon. Carefully, she unfurled the manuscript and because the writing was in some form of ancient Arabic, Haya could only read parts of it. There were many words she did not understand. Still, she could make out that the document was saying something about someone called *Yuz Asaf*.

Perhaps this paper was very valuable. Why else would someone have gone to the trouble to hide it this way? But who could she sell it to? She knew no one but the few Syrians around her. And some of them were very untrustworthy. And all of them would certainly talk. The thought occurred to her that whatever this paper was, it might bring her great misfortune. That could cause her to be arrested and ejected from Italy and stop her family from someday joining her.

Whose room was this anyway? she wondered.

Since she had arrived to work here at the college and cleaned this room, no one had been in it. Perhaps there was no around to claim this document. Perhaps it had been forgotten after the person who lived in here moved and forgot about it. Or, maybe he had died. At any rate, someone new would be occupying this room shortly.

For a moment, she thought perhaps she should just put the scroll back where she had found it and forget about it. But the inside of the plastic bag was wet now and it would ruin the document. And then the idea came to her that the safest thing of all for her was to pretend she had never discovered it. It was better to have nothing to do with this thing.

Haya violently ripped the document into little pieces. When she finished, she flushed them all down the toilet. As she started scrubbing the sink, Haya was feeling much better.

THE END

HISTORICAL NOTES

It is true that The Shroud of Turin was found by scientists to have been carbon dated incorrectly. The Vatican Commission had provided a patch sewn on it from the 14th century. It refused scientists a new dating, even excising research papers from the official report, written by medical doctors proving that the shroud exhibits blood and serum flows which only a beating heart could produce.

The *Sudarium* exists. It is the face cloth that covered the head of Jesus as he was brought down from the cross. Often during crucifixions, these cloths were placed on the heads of the crucified to spare onlookers the horror of the anguished faces. Again, the *Sudarium* shows the same fresh blood and serum flows as the Shroud. If you want to, you can go to Turin, Italy and Oviedo, Spain and see for yourself.

Even Church historians admit it was Paul who stole the most popular religion of his time (Mithraism) and overlaid it on Jesus, creating Christ the Savior and an instant version of Christianity. Among many scholars weighing in on the subject of Paul and Mithra are Friedrich Nietzsche, Sigmund Freud, Carl Jung, Soren Kierkegaard, Rev. Charles Biggs, Franz Cumont, Martin Luther, Thomas Jefferson, Martin Luther King, Christian Father Manes, Thomas Paine, to name just a few.

Ironically, St. Peter's basilica was built on top of Mithra's largest temple, which was destroyed in 320 A.D. by rampaging Christians who murdered his priests.

The early Church did attempt to destroy 56 gospels, including the first ever gospel written by St. Thomas. Some however, including that of St. Thomas and Mary Magdalene, were hidden in earthen jars and saved by monks. Only the canonically approved gospels of Mark, Matthew, Luke and John were allowed to remain in existence. Was it because those four adhered to Paul's earlier theology of Jesus the Christ redeeming the world from sin by dying on the cross?

As for the ancient Arabic (pre-Islamic) and Indian documents in the novel that describe Jesus surviving the cross, fleeing from his enemies with his mother and Mary Magdalene, and finally arriving in distant Kashmir, they're all verifiable. Each corroborate that Jesus spent time with a King Gondophares around 54 A.D, lived a long life, preached his good news and was finally being buried at the age of 80 in Srinagar.

Mary, his mother, is entombed in the nearby town of Muree, and Mary Magdalen's grave lies close by. You can go there—if you don't mind a nasty, ongoing war between Pakistan and India over the Kashmir territory.

Finally what about that organization called the Hand of Christ? Does it exist?

I combined two powerful cults, currently operating within the church. The first is *Regnum Christi,* or The Legion of Christ. It is composed of thousands of wealthy conservative Catholics, has 763 priests working in 22 countries with over 1,300 seminarians. The Legion of Christ was a favorite of the recently deceased Pope John Paul II. However, its founder, Father Marcial Maciel, stands accused of stealing millions of dollars, fathering multiple children and keeping a mistress. He also allegedly committed felonious crimes of pedophilia, drugging and raping young girls and boys, even abusing his own young seminarians, Father Maciel died in ignominy. Still, his cult flourishes.

The other organization is Opus Dei. It is a radical group, devoted solely to protecting the Church at any cost. Among its many nefarious deeds, it is accused of bombing of an Italian train killing 261 people in order to lay the blame on the Communist party so the Christian Democrats could win a Italian parliamentary election.

So what does this all add up to? Conspiracy theories? All meant to undermine and destroy Christianity?

You decide.

If you don't mind a nasty, ongoing war between Pakistan and India over the Kashmir territory, you can check out the Tomb of Jesus yourself. But a safer way would be to visit several website addresses which have received over 150 million visits.

http://www.jesus-kashmir-tomb.com/

http://www.jesus-in-india-the-movie.com/html/kashmirtomb.html

A Wikipedia article with many references on the tomb can be found on: http://en.wikipedia.org/wiki/Roza_Bal

"The Lost Tomb of Jesus" a documentary, hosted by Ted Koppel, is available for purchase on Amazon.
(Don't confuse this with the James Cameron Jerusalem film.)

An article (one of several) written by the BBC can be found at this address below. http://news.bbc.co.uk/2/hi/programmes/from_our_own_correspondent/85 87838.stm

ABOUT THE AUTHOR

John Zodrow studied for the Catholic priesthood for nine years. Since leaving, he has written motion pictures, television movies, novels and stage plays. He has opened on Broadway and recently in Europe.

NOTE FROM THE AUTHOR

Word-of-mouth is crucial for any author to succeed. If you enjoyed *The Survivor*, please leave a review online—anywhere you are able. Even if it's just a sentence or two. It would make all the difference and would be very much appreciated.

Thanks!
John Zodrow

Thank you so much for reading one of our
Christian Fiction novels.
If you enjoyed the experience, please check out our
recommended title for your next great read!

Woman in Red by Krishna Rose

"*Woman in Red - Magdalene Speaks* is a well-researched and believable work of fiction that will challenge believers and atheists with an equally rich interpretive of gospel, history, and culture of two thousand years ago."

–AUTHORS READING

View other Black Rose Writing titles at
www.blackrosewriting.com/books and use promo code
PRINT to receive a **20% discount** when purchasing.